SONS OF NIGHT

J.P. HÄKKINEN

SONS OF NIGHT

Published by: BoD™ – Books on Demand, Helsinki, Finland
Manufactured by: Books on Demand GmbH, Norderstedt, Germany
ISBN: 978-952-330-333-1

ONE

Toby was sweltering. The dark forest seemed to swallow him even though he tried to run down the path as fast as he could. Toby cursed his bad shape. F'kin fatso! Slow lump! A voice echoed from the trees. And where on earth was that annoying sound of knocking coming from? Suddenly, the ground beneath his feet turned into soft mud and his pace slowed down even more. Now Toby panicked for real. What was happening? That tapping sound kept coming closer and closer. Clearly someone was chasing him but he couldn't understand who and why.

"Toby, are you in there?" A voice was heard somewhere in the darkness.

The tapping continued. Toby tried desperately to struggle forward in the mud. He could hear the voice already beside him. Toby cried out in terror and woke up in his bed, dripping wet.

"Did we wake you up?" A sarcastic voice asked behind the ventilation window. "We agreed that we'd leave at eleven o'clock, if you remember?"

Still half-asleep, Toby groped his cell phone from the table. Indeed, it was already few minutes past eleven, he had overslept heavily. The voices

Toby heard from outside belonged to his friends, the brothers, Matty and Marc. The boys had agreed earlier that they would go to the school yard to see the destruction. The spring semester had ended last Saturday and some of the pupils had apparently celebrated the event far too boisterously. Toby tried to remember what day of the week it was today. Guess it was Thursday. On summer vacation, the days got mixed up easily.

Feeling still a bit dizzy after the abrupt waking, Toby staggered to open the window curtain. Bright daylight blinded him for a moment and he had to squint his eyes to see outside. Two grinning faces stared against him. Matty, the older of the brothers, had brown flattop hair and narrow, tanned face with deep dimples. Two years younger Marc had little longer and lighter hair and he was a head shorter than his big brother. Otherwise, the brothers were like two peas in a pod, brown and slender both.

"What happened in there?" Matty asked, chuckling. He claimed that Toby's scream had been heard all around the neighbourhood.

Toby stretched and rubbed the sleep from his eyes. He told the brothers that he had seen a terrifying nightmare. In the nightmare, for some reason, he had been in a dark forest and someone had been chasing him.

"Then your knockings and calls mixed up in the dream," Toby said, continuing that he had already thought his days were numbered, until he had woken up.

The boys burst into laughter behind the window. Matty joked that they had, if not quite a major role, then at least a side role in Toby's dream. Toby wasn't amused at all. He moaned that he had just seen the worst nightmare of his life and his friends only laughed at it. Behind the window, the laughter continued. The brothers chuckled at Toby's hair which was sticking out all over the place. They thought it looked like a spike strip. Ostentatiously, Toby threw himself back on the bed.

Matty and Marc had to press they faces up against the window to be able to see inside.

"Come on! We've got to get going!" Matty lost his temper when he saw that Toby had gone back to bed. "We need to go to the grocery store too."

"I have to have some breakfast first," Toby mumbled, face against the pillow.

The brothers wondered why anyone would eat breakfast at midday. Toby grimaced towards the window, saying he would have lunch then if it had to be so precise.

"I'll just have a quick snack," Toby promised.

Matty told Toby to hurry up, Marc and him wouldn't wait all day. Matty was about to wisecrack something about Toby's eating habits but he managed to keep his mouth shut. Toby had probably heard enough comments and taunts about his overweight already. He had been bullied at school for that matter since the first grade.

The brothers waited Toby in the front yard. The first week of summer vacation had been warm and sunny and this day was no exception. When they had left home, the thermometer had shown already for twenty-five degrees Celsius. Matty and Marc decided to sit down in the shade of the wall. The brick wall felt enjoyable cool after the cold night of early summer.

”How long will it take?” Marc asked, looking mischievously at his older brother.

”Hmm... Toby and breakfast,” thought Matty in a sarcastic tone.

Marc corrected, laughing, that it was lunch.

”Oh... right. A lunch,” Matty continued. ”I'm optimistic and say half an hour.”

Marc laughed at his brother's thoughts but stopped immediately when he saw Toby appearing in the front yard. Matty praised Toby that it was the fastest lunch he had seen in his life. Toby was still chewing food in his mouth. He recalled promising the boys that he would be quick and eat just a small portion. Marc inquired Toby what that small portion consisted.

"Chocolate cereal and a piece of cake," came the reply.

The brothers were laughing again.

"So, a small and nutritious breakfast," Matty needled. "The most important meal of the day."

Again, Marc corrected that it was Toby's lunch, not breakfast.

Toby didn't want to harp on food anymore but changed the subject, asking why the boys had knocked on the window. Because last time he checked they had a doorbell. Matty said they had assumed that Toby's Dad was in the evening shift that week. They had reckoned he could still be sleeping and would wake up to the sound of the doorbell. Toby said his Dad was up already but praised that the brothers had thought pretty nicely anyway.

"By the way," Marc suddenly urged. "How come you were still sleeping?"

"Well, it's summer vacation now, after all!" Toby grinned.

"Yeah, it is!"

Wide, happy smiles spread over all three boys' faces. The thought of two and a half months of freedom felt more than good. Although going to the school, voluntarily, seemed a bit silly, the trio still decided to go to have a look what had happened there at the weekend.

The brothers had come by bicycle so Toby fetched his bike from the garage too. Just when the boys were about to leave, the front door opened and Toby's Dad, Luke, peeked outside.

"Hello Matthew and Marcus!" Luke always used their given names.

He wondered how the brothers were so tanned already, so early in the summer, but then guessed that they had probably spend some time in the sports field. Matty and Marc admitted that that was the case. Luke glanced, smiling, at Toby who looked white as a sheet, standing beside the tanned brothers. He said the brothers should try to drag Toby to the sports field too. Toby ignored the uncomfortable subject and informed his Dad that they were going to the school. Sports and stuff could wait for better time and cooler weather. Dad reminded Toby that lunch would be at one pm, no sooner nor later. Or maybe later, but it would be served cold then. Toby promised to be back on time.

TWO

Fort Sara, the hometown of the trio of boys, was a small mill town with a population of about three thousand. Primary and secondary schools were located side by side close to the town center. Primary school pupils came from district of Fort Sara alone, but secondary school had pupils also from smaller neighboring villages. Matty, the trio's oldest, would start the sixth grade in the fall, Toby would go to the fifth grade and Marc to the fourth. At the moment, however, the boys weren't interested in studying or other school stuff. It was their summer vacation, after all.

The day before, the local newspaper had published a news where their told that there had been done some vandalism at school area. Both schools had suffered several damages. According to the report, the plantings had been partially destroyed, the shades of the lights had been smashed and the garbage cans had been overturned. The main door of the secondary school was smudged with spray paint as well. Although the boys didn't always like going to school so much, this kind of anger against the school received no understanding from them.

A sad sight met the trio at the school yard. Even though the report gave the impression that the vandalism was outrageous, they hadn't been able to imagine such a horrible view beforehand. Flower and shrub plantings were messed up totally, apparently by motocrossing over them with moped or motorcycle. Outdoor lights had been destroyed systematically and an asphalt drawing, primary school student work, was smeared by burning rubber. The trash bins had someone managed to get in right positions by then and there was no longer loose trash on the ground.

While the trio were wondering the sight at the primary school yard, a familiar figure walked towards the boys from the main door. Janitor's robust presence evoked fearful respect amongst pupils. However, behind this intimidating appearance was a fair man who was kind to the good but strict to the bad. Frank the Janitor, as the pupils called him, had a good heart. Most kids liked him and so did Toby, Matty and Marc.

”The criminal always returns to the scene of the crime!” Frank shouted from a distance, grim expression on his face.

Then he immediately flashed a mischievous smile and blinked at the boys.

”Relax, it was a joke! So, why do you guys bother coming here on your vacation?”

The boys looked at each other. Toby was usually the one who opened his mouth first in situations like this.

"We just came to see what has happened here," Toby replied.

"Yeah, some 'hard worker' has been here last weekend," Frank said, imitating quotes with his fingers.

The janitor told he had just been scraping spray paint off the main door and was on his way to lunch break. Gardeners would fix the plantings, but the lights he could fix himself when he'd have time to do it.

Frank rubbed his black stubble pensively.

"Say, guys... Do you have any idea who might be behind this?"

The trio glanced at each other again. They had a hunch alright but could they tell Frank about it. Toby cleared his throat.

"Umm, well, at least we have a good guess," Toby dodged.

"Well, probably we have the same suspects," Frank replied, continuing that the boys didn't have to give any names in case they didn't want to.

He was sorry about the fact that there was no proper evidence available. Apparently, the vandals had turned the surveillance cameras around with a long cane or something. The only thing one could see in the camera recordings was sky or plain wall.

The police had, of course, visited and taken photos of the tire tracks on the lawn but none of them alone would be useful, Frank doubted.

"Are the traces still there?" Marc dared to ask Frank the Janitor. "I thought we could also take some pictures and make investigations of our own."

Frank chuckled and shook his head. He had smoothed out the soil already and even planted new grass seed there. The plantings were still unrepaired but there the soil was so soft that there weren't any clear traces. Anyway, Frank urged the trio to keep their eyes and ears open. All new tips, which would help to catch the perpetrators, would be welcome. The boys promised to be vigilant.

"I guess it wasn't the first time something like this happened?" Toby thought.

Frank sighed and said that it really was not. Minor vandalism had been done in the past and that was why the cameras had been mounted last spring.

"But they didn't seem to help," he continued. "I guess they must be installed in a metal cage or something so that they can't be reached."

The janitor looked weary. He wiped the sweat from his forehead.

"Work is work, after all, but it's so damn hot. I envy you your summer vacation."

The boys were smiling broadly. Toby told Frank that they were about to go to the grocery.

"Maybe we'll get some ice cream and sodas, and..." Toby tempted the janitor feeling hot.

"Ok, stop that good-holiday-mooding already!" Frank interrupted and tried to look angry.

He said he was already an old man and you shouldn't be teasing old people. Nor people at any age, he added.

"Move a long, you smirking buggers!" Frank ordered playfully. "I wouldn't go hanging around in my workplace on vacation either."

The trio laughed at Frank's jesting. The janitor glanced at his watch and was already about to go to lunch break when he turned around towards the boys once again.

"Oh yeah, just remembered that Fanny was here before you came. She was, as usual, fussing around and about," Frank said with a grin. "She was going to the grocery also, so beware."

When Frank the Janitor had left, the boys stayed at the school yard for a while. Matty wondered, laughing, would they dare to go to the grocery then. Toby spat on the ground meaningfully, cursing that Fanny was the last person he wanted to bump into at the moment.

"Oh my goodness, oh my goodness!" Toby imitated Fanny's speech and gestures. "Why she has to keep snooping around! Every damn place!"

Matty and Marc laughed heartily at Toby's imitation. Matty suggested that Toby could perform a Fanny-show next Christmas celebrations at school.

"Just a grey, curly wig and glasses and a trench coat so no one would tell the difference."

Fanny was a retired school cleaner who was still continuously worried about the school and especially the pupils. All the pupils, and most of the school staff also, thought it was just too much. And annoying as heck. Frank the Janitor had once said that Fanny had appeared even in his nightmares. Her real name was Annie Fowler but the pupils had nicknamed her Fanny already years ago. Even when she was still working as a cleaner, she used to bitch about everything.

"Well, anyway, let's go to the grocery store," Matty finally said. "It's three versus one, I think we can handle one Fanny."

THREE

The grocery store was about half a kilometer away from the school. It was located in the same street as the school, called Borough Street, which run through the center of Fort Sara. Sometimes there had been three stores in Fort Sara but nowadays Weston's grocery was the only one. The city's large retail chains had forced smaller stores to shut down in Fort Sara too.

On the way to the grocery, Matty and Marc, as usual, rode like maniacs. The weather being agonizingly hot, Toby got annoyed immediately.

"Why do you always have to pedal like mad men?" Toby snapped behind the brothers. "You'll get a heat stroke or something."

Matty and Marc glanced behind and slowed down when they saw Toby's pained and, at the same time, irritated look. Matty apologized, saying that it was unintentional. Toby thought they were riding so fast solely and exclusively because they were in monster shape.

The boys were in many respects different from each other. Matty and Marc had always liked to play and do all kinds of sports and therefore were physically in top form. Toby, on the contrary, had always been a little chubby and hated sports, especially sports at school. His strengths were more mental. He was inventive and brave while the brothers, especially Marc, were more timid and cautious in many situations.

After noticing Toby's irritation, Matty led the talk back to vandalism at school.

”Would even Archie and Zac do stuff like that?”

”Well, damn sure they would!” Toby huffed. ”You can expect anything from them. The police could be notified straight off. If they compared the tire tracks with the Monkey Twins tire patterns, they would match one-to-one for sure.”

The Monkey Twins was a tough guy duo in the secondary school. The name was invented by Toby and it spring from the Monkey branded mopeds the duo used to ride. Archie had an old Honda Monkey and Zac's moped was a newer chinese copy of Honda. Both bikes, of course, were tuned up and ran like a beast. With them, the duo was terrorizing the whole town.

”Damn, if we'd have a picture of those traces!” Toby fretted.

He blustered that they could have been able to compare the tire patterns themselves and then give a tip to the police. Toby praised Marc's idea of taking pictures and said he had planned something similar activity for summer vacation.

”We would investigate and solve all kinds of suspicious things!”

”That's an awesome idea!” Marc got enthusiastic. ”We'd get some action!”

”An action? Yeah, right!” Matty laughed at his little brother's enthusiasm. ”There's enough action in SpongeBob SquarePants for you.”

”Fuck you!”

”Oh my goodness,” Toby began to imitate Fanny again. ”That's terrible language! Shame on you!”

A little verbal brawl between the brothers ended in uncontrollable laughter. Marc laughed so hard that he drifted to the road verge and almost hit the Weston's banner stand. With a quick steering maneuver, he somehow got back on the road.

”Hey, there's popsicles on sale today!” Marc yelled casually as if nothing had happened.

Matty and Toby laughed at Marc's twists with tears in their eyes. They marveled how he had still managed to read the banner in that hassle. Laughing, the trio turned into the driveway. Toby spotted first the familiar looking rollator which was parked near the entrance.

”Speak of the devil. It's Fanny's rollator all right. I so hoped that she would have gone home by now.”

The boys parked their bicycles beside Fanny's rollator. Marc suggested, grinning, that they should let the air out of her tires. Toby shot down the suggestion immediately. He said they wouldn't lower themselves to the Monkey Twins level, under any circumstances. Even if Fanny was annoying as heck. Matty agreed with Toby, saying that the they were the good guys, not the bad ones.

Suddenly, the automatic sliding door of the store opened. All three turned their heads towards the entrance. They were relieved when they saw just a mother with a small child coming from the store, instead of Fanny.

"Boy, are we nervous or what!" Matty chuckled. "Come on, let's go now! She won't eat us!"

A pleasant coolness surged towards the boys as they entered the grocery store. They couldn't see any sign of Fanny or other customers. The boys walked through the fruit and vegetable section and went directly to the ready meals aisle. Matty and Marc had planned to have pizza for lunch.

"Didn't your Mom make lunch ready for you?" Toby teased. "So, now you have to eat unhealthy ready meal."

Matty patted his flat belly and replied that he and Marc could afford it.

"How about you? Ice cream, soda and candy, or what did you say to Frank."

It was just joking, Toby excused, he was going to buy only that cheap popsicle Marc had spotted. He claimed he was about to start a diet from that day on. The brothers laughed at Toby's diet talks. They recalled hearing something similar coming from his mouth before, without noticeable results.

"I really am surprised if you manage to get past the candy shelf with empty hands," Matty yet blurted.

"It's a piece of cake!" Toby insisted. "And no pun intended!"

The brothers got their pizzas and the trio headed to the freezer cabinets to get the popsicles. Even then, there was no sign of Fanny anywhere.

Toby opened the freezer door and began to poke around the assortment.

"Let's see what flavors we have in here? Pineapple and strawberry, at least."

Marc and Matty were peeking over Toby's shoulder.

"Give me the strawberry. What about Matty, which one..."

The trio of boys were so focused to select the popsicles that none of them had noticed the approaching danger. Fanny had appeared out of nowhere behind the boys.

"What's going on in here?" Anger could be heard in Fanny's creaking voice. "Why do you keep the freezer door open needlessly! Oh, my goodness sake! Have you not been taught that you must choose *before* you open the freezer door."

The boys froze with fear. Toby recovered from the shock first and slammed the door shut.

"But you couldn't see them," Toby tried to defend himself. "And the door wasn't open that..."

"No buts and excuses!" Fanny did not let Toby finish the sentence.

She complained something about the present day youths who had no manners. Always had to be correcting, she claimed.

The boys' faces turned as red as a fire truck as they were listening Fanny's preaching. They frantically thought how to get out of the unpleasant situation. Finally, Fanny snorted audibly and moved on towards the cash desk, mumbling herself.

"Crazy old hag!" Toby barked in a low voice as Fanny disappeared behind the shelves. "Let's take the goddamn popsicles and leave!"

"Is it safe to go there yet?" Marc hesitated. "She's at the cash desk by now and it takes time."

"I'm not going stand here and wait because of that old witch!" Toby almost trembled with rage.

Matty agreed and said that they wouldn't be dodging Fanny. It would make them feel only more guilty even if they had done nothing wrong. The trio picked up the popsicles from the freezer and headed to the cash desk.

Storekeeper Weston himself was behind the cash register and was just serving Fanny. Boldly, Toby in front, the boys went in line behind the woman. Fanny glared at them over her glasses.

"Someone had been vandalizing the school again last weekend," Fanny tried to goad Mr. Weston into gossiping. "Raging like madmen around the school yard. God knows, what hell machines they had been riding."

"So I heard," the storekeeper didn't seem interested in discussing the subject with Fanny.

Fanny didn't give up so easily. She complained about the youngsters who tend to goof around more and more. She was worried where the world was going.

"Oh, my goodness!"

Looking deadpan, the storekeeper was scanning Fanny's shopping with the reader device and didn't even glance at her.

"Well, the schools were out on Saturday, it's always a bit like that," Mr. Weston tried to soften the issue.

He yet added that fortunately it's only a small group of young people who tend to do such things.

"People didn't act like that in the old days," Fanny continued whining and glanced towards the boys again. "No one has even taught those three that..."

"It makes twenty-three and fifty, Thank You," Mr. Weston interrupted Fanny's lecture.

For a moment, there was a great silence as Fanny had to focus on using the card terminal. However, her face expression indicated that she was annoyed for not having any response from the storekeeper. Mr. Weston peeked at the boys and was speaking silently. "She's plain crazy," the boys could read from his lips. The trio had to hold back laughter. The storekeeper was, indeed, a nice guy.

Fanny got the payment done and didn't say a word anymore. Mr. Weston wished Fanny a good day in an overly polite voice as he already began to serve the boys. Meanwhile, Fanny was packing her shopping in a hurry and when done, she immediately rushed out of the store. Mr. Weston sighed spontaneously as the doors slid shut.

"Man, how can someone be so bitter and negative all the time!" he wondered.

"She has had to tolerate badly behaving children for forty years," Toby wisecracked.

"Oh yeah," Mr. Weston laughed. "Well, that explains it!"

The shopkeeper had school-aged children himself and therefore he very well knew Fanny's reputation and history. In fact, Mr. Weston even belonged to the parents association in primary school.

"To be honest, it was quite a nasty sight at the school yard," Mr. Weston turned serious.

He said that, in the sense, he understood Fanny's irritation.

The boys nodded.

"Yeah, we just came from there and saw it."

Mr. Weston told the boys that the parents association had planned to form some kind of patrol system. The patrol groups would be formed of the parents who volunteer to patrol in the nighttime, mostly on weekends. The patrol groups would try to prevent vandalism and other disruptive behavior at school and, if necessary, elsewhere in the town too. One patrol would consist of four or five adults and there would be at least three groups which would patrol in shifts.

"But it's only in the planning stage," Mr. Weston said. "The patrols would be ready by autumn, at the soonest."

Matty and Marc noticed how Toby obviously had something in his mind. He had a mysterious hint of a smile on his face. The brothers guessed their friend had got some brilliant idea when Mr. Weston was talking. The storekeeper wished them a good vacation, the trio thanked him and hurried their way out.

Fortunately for the boys, Fanny had already rolled on her way. Toby was smiling like a small child on Christmas morning. He was just waiting for the brothers to ask first. Matty and Marc didn't ask immediately, though, but wanted to tease Toby a little. They were just rustling the popsicles out of the wrapping papers.

"Come on, spit it out," Matty finally persuaded. "What do you got in mind?"

"I got a monster idea in there!" Toby made the most out of the situation.

"You don't say!" Marc blurted.

He demanded Toby to tell, at last, what invention to save the world he had invented. Toby ignored Marc's sarcasm and continued ceremoniously that he got the idea from what Mr. Weston had said. About that parents patrol thing, that was. Again, Toby took a break, looking important. He sucked his popsicle and looked at the brothers in turn.

"Okay, so?" Matty was already getting frustrated.

"We will begin to do that!" Toby's expression was triumphant.

The brothers looked at each other in confusion.

"To do what?" Matty wondered. "Patrolling?"

"That's right!" Toby seemed to wait for applause but continued when nothing happened.

His majestic idea was that the three of them, Toby, Matty and Marc, would begin to take care of law and order in Fort Sara. By night. Toby didn't have the patience to wait for the brothers' reactions anymore but revealed the whole idea right away.

"Marc here, was looking for some action, and I myself had similar thoughts too. So, here we have some action. We shall patrol at school area and even elsewhere in the town, by night. We will prevent vandalism and other crimes. We could even establish some kind of a secret society and..."

At this stage, Matty cut Toby's monologue. He told Toby to take it easy and catch some breath or something. Matty wondered how they, three whippersnappers, could possibly prevent vandalism, not to mention the real crimes.

"You should have let me finish!" Now Toby, in turn, lost his temper.

"Yeah, but it will surely fail because of that night thing alone," announced Marc his opinion for the matter. "Our parents won't let us wander around in the middle of the night, no way."

"But we won't be asking any permissions to do so," Toby announced triumphantly and got excited again.

He visioned that the trio would just leave, not telling anyone. In summer, it wouldn't even be a problem. They could sleep in a tent or even in their hut and sneak out at night, without anyone noticing their departure. At the moment, the ideas seemed to flow out of Toby's head.

"Maybe the hut could act as a headquarters for our secret society!"

Matty and Marc glanced at each other. That didn't sound so bad after all, when thought through.

"We'll operate in secrecy and give tips to the police anonymously..." Toby continued his brainstorming and fantasizing.

Little by little, the brothers began to warm to Toby's ideas. Marc joked that Toby's plans sounded like real action all right. Matty laughed that there might be enough excitement for him too.

"So, we will establish a secret society which will be operating at night," Matty began to gather all the ideas together which Toby had presented in a hurry. "And in secrecy, i.e. we try to stay invisible."

"Exactly!" Toby replied. "And the intention is, of course, to stop the vandalism and other criminal activity. For example, by giving anonymous tips to the police."

For a moment, the boys looked at each other, smiling mysteriously. Marc praised that the idea seemed better and better all the time. Toby, the father of the idea, barely managed to keep his feet on the ground. The trio imagined all kinds of exciting night adventures that lay ahead. Their dreaming was interrupted by Matty's cellphone ringing.

"It's Mom!" Matty informed the others. "She's going to ask our eating situation, I reckon."

Matty guessed it right. After a quick exchange of words, he managed to convince his Mom that the brothers' nutritional things were in order.

"Always worrying!" Matty groused after the call.

Toby thought that mothers tend to do so. He said it was only a good thing if someone was taking care of you.

"I guess it is," Matty admitted but said he also thought that parents should trust their children a bit. If they promised to do something, they usually would do it.

"Like being home at lunch time," Toby said, glancing at his watch. "I promised to be home by one pm and it's already ten to one."

"Well, let's go then before your Dad calls," Matty laughed.

The trio jumped on wheels and rode on their way. Toby had to ride with the popsicle in his mouth because he hadn't had time to eat it yet. Matty thought it was a miracle which, however, was explained by the fact that Toby had spoken so much that he had not had time to suck his popsicle. Toby told Matty to suck something else. Marc chuckled at the duo's verbal battle and thought it would be good to stop now when it was a tie. Toby and Matty agreed the result was fair enough.

Matty and Marc decided to ride by Toby's home on Meadow Street even though it wasn't the shortest way for them. The boys rode side by side and continued chatting about the secret society and the night patrols.

"We must keep the formation meeting of the secret society already today," Toby enthused. "Are you free in the evening?"

Both Matty and Marc said they had no plans for the night, so the boys agreed to meet at the hut at six pm. Toby promised to check beforehand if the hut was okay after the winter, at least it had to be cleaned up.

The boys said goodbyes to each other at Meadow Street and headed for their respective homes. The trio's thoughts circled already around the exciting summer adventures ahead.

FOUR

A musty smell flooded out of the hut as Toby opened the door. It had been tightly closed over the winter. For what Toby could see, the hut had seemed to be okay from outside, though. The location of the hut was ideal for the operations of the secret society. It was located near the border of the property with a thick wooded park on the other side of the border. The distance between the hut and the house, Toby's home, was only twenty meters but only the windows of the storage were faced to the hut. Toby thought it would be easy to slip unnoticed through the park at night.

The hut was originally built by Toby's big brother William and his friends. Willie had already other interests nowadays so Toby, Matty and Marc had taken the hut for their own use. The hut was built beside a thick-branched pine. Initially, the hut had been only on the branches of the pine but it had been expanded later. The expansion part reached to the ground, so there were kind of upper and lower decks in the hut now.

Toby let his eyes wander around the lower deck. The ceiling, which was, at the same time, the upper deck floor, seemed to be alright as well as the flooring. Toby noticed that he could just barely stand up straight in the hut. Last summer, his head wasn't even close to touch the ceiling. Matty would no longer be able to stand straight in here, Toby figured.

Next to the tree trunk was a small opening in the ceiling, which could be climbed through to the upper deck. The cut branches acted as a ladder. Toby climbed up just to see how it looked like in the upper deck. He peeked through the opening and could smell that the mustiness was much stronger there. Toby noticed that they had forgotten the foam paddings on the floor over the winter. Upstairs, as well as downstairs, there was one window facing to the house. The pieces of foam below the window seemed tarnished. Toby concluded that snow and rain had fallen through the window on top of the paddings.

Toby climbed higher and tried to heave himself through the small opening to the upper deck. Bloody hell, is this hole getting smaller or am I getting bigger? Toby cussed. He could already see the headlines before his eyes: "11-year-old boy got stuck inside a hut - the fire brigade had to release the victim". I have to consider that diet thing, seriously, Toby thought as he pulled himself with great difficulty in the upstairs. He looked around and realized he had to be on his knees, otherwise he would hit his head in the ceiling. The hut was roughly square-shaped and slightly less than two meters long so Toby figured that the trio could very well sleep upstairs, on the floor.

Soon turned out that the musty odor came from the foam paddings, as Toby had reckoned. He decided to air and dry all the pieces out in the sun right away. Toby was going to throw the paddings out of the window and began with the dirtiest piece. He forced it through the window and dropped it down.

"Eww, what the fuck?" Outside, Willie's voice sounded both surprised and angry. "What the hell are you playing at?"

Toby peeked from the window, looked down and saw his brother arranging his hair back in order.

"I'm sorry, I didn't know you were there," Toby expressed regret while holding back laughter. "I intended to air and dry these paddings, they were exposed to water and smelled a little bit."

"Oh, a little bit!" replied Willie, still annoyed. "That piece was, at least, as wet as a dishrag and smelled like shit."

Willie brushed his hair once again and smelled his fingers, ensuring that the smell wasn't stuck in his hair. He asked curiously why Toby was sweeping the hut.

"Matty and Marc will be here in the evening," Toby replied vaguely, trying not to reveal too much of their plans. "We'll sleep in here sometimes, perhaps."

Overnight in the hut seemed to draw Willie's interest. He told Toby that he and his buddies had also slept upstairs sometimes and it had been awesome. There was just enough room there for three kids to sleep, Willie said. A hint of a smile passed Willie's lips as he was thinking back his own overnights in the hut. He claimed they had slept quietly in the hut all night but Toby wasn't buying it. Certainly Willie and his friends had had night adventures of their own.

The brothers were like night and day. Willie was sporty-looking, although his sports were limited to the occasional hanging around the gym. Toby was a dreamer and liked to read books and comics, Willie was a more practical person and handy with tools. In addition, he was interested in all motor powered vehicles while Toby was more interested in computers and games. However, despite all the differences and the six-year age gap between the brothers, they got along very well with each other. Toby admired his older brother. Willie had always stood up for him when he was being bullied and helped a lot in other things too.

Willie glanced his brand new motorbike standing in the driveway. He told that he was going for a little ride but promised to come back before eight so Toby wouldn't have to be alone all night.

Toby, feeling uncomfortable, scratched the sun-warmed pine resin from the window frames. Willie had been a little overprotective since their parents had divorced.

"I'll be fine, don't worry," Toby assured. "Besides, like I said, Matty and Marc are coming here in the evening."

Willie was already about to leave when Toby tried to ask him where he was going. Willie didn't seem to want to reveal everything but said he was going to Lake Goblin, at least. Maybe he would go even for a swim if the water wasn't too cold. Toby suspected that he would go to see Joanna also but Willie didn't admit that, he just smiled mysteriously.

Toby looked at the window as Willie was kick-starting his motorbike. Willie had gotten his driving license earlier in the spring, the bike was bought already in the winter. Dad had paid half of both, the license and the bike. They had apparently some sort of a deal that Willie would be doing some tasks at home, firewood and stuff like that, in return. The bike finally started and Willie accelerated away.

The afternoon's blazing sun had heated the hut agonizingly hot. Toby dropped the rest of the foam pieces down and pushed himself through the narrow opening back downstairs. As he got out of the hut, he put the pieces in the sun to air and dry.

Then he settled down for a moment and gave himself a well-deserved rest in the shadow of the pine.

In the forest, just behind the hut, was a path which went through the park in the direction of the school and the town center. Toby thought the hut would fit perfectly for their purposes. In the darkness of the night you could easily sneak out along the path and go patrolling. Toby walked through the route to the school in his mind. Along the path to Meadow Street, a little way to the north, then the walkway to the left, cross Rowan Street and straight to the alley, along the path through the park...

"What are you, Toby, dreaming about?" Dad had snuck around the corner of the hut while Toby was planning the route.

"Umm, nothing," Toby replied quickly. "I was feeling hot while cleaning so I'm just resting a little."

Dad didn't ask anything about the cleaning. He had just come to tell Toby that he was about to go to work.

Explosives factory Kermia Ltd. had operated in Fort Sara for more than seventy years until it was closed down about three years ago. The factory had employed almost a thousand people at its best which was about a half of the town's population. Actually, the whole town had once grown around the factory and, in most of the families, at least one parent had worked there. Toby's Dad had also worked at Kermia until it was closed down. Now he, like many other citizens of Fort Sara, had found work in the city. Toby had used to his Dad's shift work, and thus irregular rhythm of life, already when Dad was still working at Kermia.

Dad told Toby that he had been in talks with Mom about the summer vacation arrangements. Toby was annoyed by his parents' arrangements and replied that he had his own plans for the summer too.

"Well, let's see later on, who's doing what and where," Dad soothed. "Willie promised to come home before eight so you don't need to be alone all night."

"Yeah, yeah, I know that already!" Toby retorded. "I'll manage on my own already!"

Dad said he wasn't, in no way, doubting that. When Toby told that Matty and Marc were coming, Dad reminded them to behave themselves and to stay away from stupidity. That Toby promised.

After Dad had left for work, Toby decided to go inside for a rest, waiting for the great night.

FIVE

"Welcome to the formation meeting of the secret society," announced Toby with an official tone in his voice. "The subject of the meeting is, therefore, establishment of a secret society which will prevent vandalism and other crimes in Fort Sara. I declare the meeting open."

"What the hell was that?" Matty wondered with amusement. "This isn't some formal meeting anyway."

"Well, in any case, the meeting must be opened," Toby defended himself.

Matty and Marc had arrived slightly early to the hut. Toby had just been placing the foam paddings back into their places so the brothers had had a chance to help him with that. Both of them had agreed with Toby that the hut was a perfect place for their society. At first, however, they needed to get the secret society officially launched.

The trio had climbed upstairs and sat in a circle on top of the cushions. The musty odor no longer existed and the upper floor had suitably cooled down since the afternoon. The day had turned into evening. The excitement and enthusiasm amongst the boys were almost tangible at the beginning of the first meeting.

"If I would, however, act as some kind of a chairman," Toby suggested gently.

It was okay for the brothers and Matty mentioned that the whole idea had been Toby's, after all. Matty asked Toby to be Toby, though, not imitating some real chairman. Toby promised to be himself.

Chairman Toby started the meeting by repeating the purpose of the secret society they were about to form. The purpose was to prevent vandalism and other suspicious activities at school and elsewhere in the town. After that, Toby told about the nature of the activity. Its main theme would be patrolling the school and the town, mainly on weekend nights. The operation would be performed in secrecy and, by all possible means, avoid being revealed. Also, during the day, they would keep their eyes open and operate as much as possible. The hut would act as the headquarters and mainly from there they would leave for their night patrols.

"Are there any questions at this stage?" Toby understood to stop his monologue.

Matty teased Toby on purpose and raised his hand like in school. Toby, in turn, very teacher-like encouraged Matty to ask his question.

"Main theme, mainly, main, main, main..." Matty ragged. "Are you, perhaps, the main man?"

Toby said he could be the president, the chairman, and the main man of their secret society, if necessary. Matty wouldn't have to be worried about that at all.

"Did you have any *real* questions?" The chairman didn't let Matty's joking distract him.

"How long are we going to do this patrolling thing?" asked Matty immediately.

"I've thought that, at least, now on summer vacation and possibly during other holiday periods too," Toby replied and continued. "If you recall, the parents will begin to run their own operations in autumn. Then we won't be able to continue anymore."

At this point, Marc also raised his hand for a question.

"Oh god dammit, what's the matter with you?" Toby got angry. "We're not at school, so if you have something to ask, then ask! You don't need my permission to speak."

Marc wanted to know how would they, three brats, succeed in this kind of action. In practice, he meant. Toby's idea was that they would keep hiding and give anonymous tips to the police who would take care of the rest. In addition, they would write down descriptions and other eyewitness sightings for future reference. Marc was still worried about getting the permission from the parents to sleep in the hut. Matty was sure that it wouldn't be a problem because of the summer vacation. Matty, in turn, was concerned about the hiding thing. How would they, for example, get to the school yard without anyone noticing it? Toby assured it would succeed and told that he had even planned the route earlier in the day. Also, patrolling in the town shouldn't cause any problems, Toby believed. There were no more questions.

"Now it's time for the highlight of this meeting and a historic moment is at hand," Toby continued the meeting solemnly.

"Every society has a name, right? So, our secret society must have one too."

Again, typically for him, Toby paused to underline the specificity of the situation and glanced brothers in turn. Matty got annoyed again by Toby's showing off.

"Of course you have the name ready, right?"

"No I haven't. This name thing crossed my mind just a little while ago," Toby explained. "But, in my opinion, the name should be somewhat punchy and, perhaps, a little scary."

Soon-to-be members of the secret society began to consider possible names silently in their minds, as the Chairman Toby had proposed. Toby had ordered five minutes thinking time. Everyone should come up with one name proposal and the best name among them would be chosen by voting. Own proposal, of course, you weren't allowed to vote. Matty had been interested to know what would happen if there was a tie of votes. Toby had ordered that the chairman's vote would then break the tie. Matty had accepted this, stating again that Toby was, indeed, behind all this secret society thing.

"Time's up!" Toby announced.

"Argh, I didn't have enough time to come up with anything," Matty agonized and figured that he had left his brain at school.

"Well, tough shit," Toby replied rudely. "Then we'll choose the name among Marc's and my proposals."

Suddenly, Marc realized it would be then Matty who would choose the name in this situation. Because Toby could only vote for his proposal and he himself only Toby's. Matty began to laugh hysterically at the situation. Toby, instead, wasn't amused but complained that Matty was an unimaginative lagger.

"A lagger, who will decide the name, though!" Matty replied, still laughing uncontrollably.

Marc told his brother to calm down so they could carry on. Toby continued as a chairman of the meeting, ignoring Matty's chuckle.

"My own proposition for the name of our secret society is Commando Trio. I now ask member Marc to tell his proposition."

Looking embarrassed, Marc glanced at the two older members of the secret society. Being suddenly in the center of attention felt awkward for the youngest of the trio.

"Come on, spit it out!" rushed Matty his younger brother.

"This is probably pretty stupid, but..." began Marc gently. "From the word scary came to mind some motorcycle gang, like Sons of Anarchy, and when our action would take place mainly at night..." Marc hesitated again.

"Well, I suggest the name Sons of Night."

For a moment, there was dead silence in the hut. Marc looked cautiously at the boys. Toby and Matty looked first at each other and then at Marc.

"Sons of Night," Matty broke the silence. "Holy shit, where did that come from? What an awesome name if you ask me! Well, you *do* ask me," Matty laughed.

"Yeah, that's a great name!" Toby also admitted. "And a lot better than mine, really."

Massive plaudits from the boys made Marc blush. In particular, the plaudits from his big brother felt good. Toby guessed there weren't any doubts about the name of their secret society. Matty admitted that the choice was clear and there wasn't even any bias. Toby announced that the name of their secret society was now officially Sons of Night and the society was hence formed. Then, Chairman Toby announced the formal portion of the meeting closed.

Matty suggested that they should celebrate this historic event in some way. Toby and Marc agreed. Toby suggested having sodas and doughnuts at Ace One which received unanimous support. At Ace One, they could also plan Sons of Night's first mission.

Cheerful and enthusiastic trio exited from the headquarters and headed to Ace One.

SIX

Ace One, where the boys had chosen to celebrate the forming of Sons of Night, was the only gas station and, at the same time, the only cafe in Fort Sara. It was about two kilometers away from Toby's home. The gas station located near the highway leading to the city, at the crossing of Fort Sara Road and Powder Mill Street. When approaching from the highway, Fort Sara was on the right along Fort Sara Road. On the opposite direction, when turning to Powder Mill Street, was located closed Kermia's explosives factory about half a mile away. The factory had been built far away from the center of Fort Sara for safety reasons. Possible explosion accident would have caused destruction over a wide area. Beyond the open fields, the huge factory area with its numerous chimneys could be seen all the way from the gas station. Smoke was no longer rising to the sky from the chimneys, otherwise the landscape appeared the same as always. However, the members of newly formed Sons of Night were not interested in the factory at that moment.

The sun had slowly began to set towards the horizon as the boys turned from Fort Sara Road into the driveway. Despite the cooling evening, the air shimmered in the distance above the fields. Once again Toby had had to point out the brothers about the speed during the trip. Matty had replied that it would do only good for Toby to get winded at times. Toby hadn't said anything back but, in his mind, he agreed with that. It had just been so annoying when Matty had said it.

The trio parked their bikes on the bike rack against the wall of the gas station and marched inside. There were no other customers in the cafe but the regulars who seemed to be sitting there all the time. Those four geezers turned to look at who was coming. When they realized that the boys were locals, they lost their interest and carried on sitting.

Ace One owner's daughter Joanna, with whom Willie had obviously something going on, was behind the cafe counter. Not that Willie had admitted it directly but the boys had concluded it themselves. Even the boys thought that Joanna seemed to be a nice girl, really. At least, she was always friendly when they visited Ace One and greeted them also when they came across in town. Even now, Joanna had immediately greeted them cheerfully as they entered the cafe.

On the way to Ace One, Toby had suggested that for Marc, as the father of the name Sons of Night, he and Matty would offer the goodies. Matty had agreed and Marc had been very honored by this special recognition. All the boys chose the same luscious jelly doughnuts. And for a drink, Marc chose apple soda while Matty and Toby chose cola. Toby fancied also chocolate bars next to the cash register but controlled himself because the brothers started to needle him immediately.

"Hey guys!" Joanna greeted the boys once again at the counter. "Is someone having a birthday or something?"

"Well, sort of, but it's a secret," Toby said cautiously, without revealing the reason for the celebration.

"Okay, well, then I won't ask further," Joanna laughed and winked at the boys. "We all *do* have our secrets."

"Me and Matty will pay for Marc," Toby explained to Joanna. "He has kind of deserved it."

Joanna decided to scan the trio's items separately in the cash register, then Matty and Toby were able to pay Marc's share for half.

After paying, the boys walked to the furthest window table, far away from the geezers, so they could talk about Sons of Night and its missions in peace. The doughnuts disappeared and soda bottles emptied in no time and the talk soon turned to the future adventures. Toby suggested they should start the operations already on the weekend. Matty and Marc agreed and said the coming weekend would be ok for them. The boys decided that the first mission would take place already the next day or, being precise, at night.

”Action starts tomorrow!” Toby enthused.

Matty began to laugh again at Marc's talks about the action earlier in the day and couldn't resist teasing his little brother for it.

”Well, let's see who's laughing at night!” Marc blustered. ”I think Matty will shit his pants already before sunset!”

The brothers shot verbal arrows at each other for a while until a high-pitched engine sound, coming from the yard, interrupted the bickering.

”Dammit!” Toby cursed as he glanced outside. ”The Monkey Twins! Why did they have to come here just now!”

The school's badass duo had been bullying and agitating Toby countless times. Fortunately, the duo had moved to high school in the previous autumn but during the free time, the situation hadn't changed. You could see fear and anxiety on Toby's face. Matty and Marc hadn't been picked on by the Monkey Twins but the duo surely caused fear in them too.

”Let's just wait in here and see if they go away,” Matty tried to calm down the situation.

Toby didn't think they would be so lucky.

”They came to fill up those piece of shit machines and when they come in to pay, they will spot us for sure. It's better for us to go out right away, then we might be able to sneak away while they are fuelling. For fuck's sake, why they had to come!"

The trio decided to try to leave unnoticed but the attempt failed before it had really started. As soon as the boys stepped out of the door, one of the boys, wearing a helmet, looked up.

"Well, well, well, look who's waddling," Zac's voice sounded unclear because of the helmet. However, the sarcastic tone in his voice was clear alright. "Tubby-Tobias and his friends."

Toby's real name was Tobias but only enemies and strangers called him that.

The other half of the Monkey Twins also woke up to the situation.

"Yup, it's Chubby-Toby alright," Archie followed his friend. "And of course, face covered with sugar. From a doughnut, I assume?"

"Close but no sugar," Zac laughed. "No, wait, there's plenty of it!"

The duo burst into laughter at their own clumsy jokes. Unfortunately, the boys' bicycles were standing right in front of the gas pumps, so leaving the situation was difficult. The trio frozen on the spot and didn't know what to do.

Suddenly, in the direction of the factory was heard the sound of the approaching motorcycle. The Monkey Twins stopped their mocking and turned to look at who was coming. Four-stroke engine purred at idle as Willie turned his bike into the driveway. Suddenly, The Monkey Twins had lost their interest in teasing the boys and looked, instead, a little jumpy.

Seeing his little brother and his buddies, Willie raised his hand to greet them.

"Hi, what's up chiefs?" Willie asked as he shut off his motorcycle. At the same time, he realized who was at the gas pumps and noticed also the tense situation.

"Aha, and here the Monkey Twins are bullying again!" Willie pushed his bike against Zac's front wheel.

"Don't you morons get it!" Willie raged. "Leave Toby and his buddies alone! Or do I have to teach you a lesson?"

Zac and Archie seemed to have forgotten refuelling and were kick-starting their mopeds in a hurry. Only black smoke and the stench of oil remained as the monkey duo speeded away. Willie guessed that now a lesson wouldn't be necessary but even those idiots' IQs would be sufficient this time. Toby seemed relieved as the incident came to an end unexpectedly.

"They forgot to fill up," Matty chuckled, also relieved.

"I hope they'll run out of gas, as far from home as possible," Willie smirked. "In this heat, they're sweating like pigs, pushing those piece of junk back home."

Willie wanted to know more about the incident, what had that been all about? Looking embarrassed, Toby kicked stones on the ground and replied it was the same thing as always.

"Those two... always mocking."

Willie thought it would be better to ignore all their insults. Those two were just projecting their own bad feelings to others. He thought it would then be more severe if bullying was also physical, even though he admitted that words could hurt badly too.

"What brought you here, by the way?" Willie changed the subject as he was placing his motorcycle on its side stand.

You could see how proud he was of his Husqvarna-branded motorcycle. The bike was an enduro which was nice to ride on trails of woods. The boys didn't reveal the real reason for being there, they just said they were celebrating the summer holiday. Even Willie's question had been, perhaps, a mere formality because he immediately changed the subject back to his bike and riding it. He had been riding near the factory, in the woods of Lake Goblin, where innumerable trails were crisscrossing everywhere. The place was perfect for enduro, Willie praised.

"How does the bike feel?" asked Matty politely, acting like he was interested.

"Just awesome," Willie got even more excited. "In the four-stroke engine there's enough power even at low RPM."

The boys weren't much interested in motorcycle technology, and they understood almost nothing about it either, but the bike itself sure looked good, though. Willie told also that he had swum in Lake Goblin and the water had been warm enough. He recommended a little swimming trip for the boys too.

"By the way, I had a serious close call at that crossroads near the lake," Willie suddenly remembered. "Back there, where Lake Goblin Road meets the factory service road. A car came along the service road and just drove through the Give Way sign and came straight in front of me. I had to lock the brakes up and almost fell off."

Willie got excited as he was thinking back the incident and you could tell by the tone of his voice that it really had been a dangerous situation. Toby, of course, became immediately interested and asked more details about the car.

"It was a red van. Ford Transit or something. A rusty piece of shit anyway."

"Did you see the license plate?" Toby was already imaging Sons of Night chasing a mysterious van.

”No, un-fuckin-fortunately,” Willie cursed. ”It came so fast and there was a terrible dust cloud behind it.”

Willie complained that if he had fallen, his Husqvarna would be all scratched up now. He said he would want to have a word or two with the driver.

”So, if you guys happen to see that red Transit somewhere around here, please let me know.”

The trio promised to keep their eyes open. Then Willie yet remembered that there had been another guy in the van too, besides the driver. This co-driver had held on to the grab handle with his right hand. Willie remembered this because the guy had had a huge tattoo on his arm.

”It was a skull or something,” Willie recalled. ”Horrible anyway.”

The boys glanced at each other surreptitiously. This could be the first mission for Sons of Night even if they had to operate in daylight. Toby was already creating a strategy in his mind. They could monitor the traffic in Fort Sara, along the highway, both incoming and outgoing.

”Is Joanna at work?” Willie asked, waking the boys from their dreams.

”Yup,” replied Toby, smiling. ”Why?”

”That's none of your business!”

Willie was of the opinion that the boys were too young to understand that kind of stuff. He grinned and said they would be ready in a few years to come, though. Willie suggested it was about time for the boys to go home. It was bedtime for mommy's little sunshines, anyway, he teased. The boys told Willie where to get off as he was walking inside to meet Joanna. Anyway, they took their bikes and rode off towards home. On the way, Toby opened a conversation about the forthcoming missions of Sons of Night.

"Tomorrow we will go to monitor the traffic."

"Where do you suggest we should go?" Matty asked.

"To Rocky Hill. Up there, where the road cut is, you can see the highway in both directions," Toby explained.

He also suggested they should take binoculars along so they would be able to see even better. Marc said he had small and handy binoculars which he could take along. Toby said it would be good because, if he remembered right, they didn't even have binoculars of any kind.

Matty wanted to know what would happen if they saw the van. Toby decided they would write down the license plate number, at least. And if the van turned towards Fort Sara, they would go after and search for it.

"Okay, well, what if we catch it?" Matty yet asked. "Are we going to call Willie?"

"No, I thought that we should leave them some kind of a warning note," Toby grinned. "Like, stop that speeding or Sons of Night will come and stop it."

The brothers thought it was a great idea. Marc was already planning that they should give warnings to other speeders as well. Instead of speeding tickets, they would put warning notes on cars' windshields. Toby thought, however, that it would be too dangerous, Sons of Night would be revealed right away.

The boys decided not to leave to Rocky Hill until midday of the following day so the brothers wouldn't have to wake Toby up again. It was also decided to take packed lunches and sleeping pads along. Toby suggested also a swimming trip after the traffic monitoring mission. Matty liked the idea but Marc said he was going to football practice in the evening and wouldn't make it to the swimming trip. Toby reminded the brothers that they must get the permission from their parents for sleeping in the hut. The boys said they would remember and would surely get the permission too.

At the Meadow Street junction, the trio parted ways as Toby headed for his home. From a distance, Toby yet shouted, reminding Matty to take swimming suit and goggles along. A story was told that there was something exciting beneath the surface of Lake Goblin.

SEVEN

Rugged Rocky Hill was standing tall on the northern edge of Fort Sara. On the west side of the hill, the highway leading to the city cut the lower ridge of the hill in half. From the top of the road cut you could get a good view down to the highway and all the way to the intersection of Fort Sara. The gas station Ace One, instead, was hidden behind the hill as the highway curved slightly at that point.

Before heading to Rocky Hill, the boys had gathered together at the hut. At the headquarters, they had done plans for the day and for the forthcoming night patrol. The brothers had received the permission, as expected, although their Mom had worried again a little too much. Toby had just announced to his Dad that he was going to sleep in the hut and it had been ok, just like that.

Everything had been planned carefully for the night of adventure, including the clothing. Matty had pointed out that even though the days were sultry, the nights of early summer weren't necessarily very warm. Toby had agreed. He had checked the weather forecast and, according to that, the temperature would drop even below ten degrees Celsius at night. The boys had also decided to wear dark clothes so that they would merge into the dark night as well as possible. In addition, Toby had come up with the idea that they should wear balaclavas so their pale faces wouldn't reveal them. At least, he himself was so fair-haired and pale that his head would shine like a lighthouse in the night. Matty and Marc wouldn't have the same problem being so tanned and dark haired but the brothers had decided to get balaclavas anyway. Toby already had a store-bought balaclava but Matty and Marc would try to make ones from old knit caps.

However, at the moment, Sons of Night was accomplishing its mission of the day which was to hunt down the red van that had almost run over Willie the day before. The boys had left their bikes at the foot of Rocky Hill, at the beginning of the jogging path. The lighted jogging path ran around Rocky Hill and cycling wasn't allowed on it. The boys had obeyed the rule dutifully even though the jogging path had already seen its best days. Weeds were growing everywhere and only a narrow footpath was left in the middle. Almost no one used the path for jogging anymore, but in winter, there were still a lot of enthusiastic cross-country skiers skiing on the trail. However, at that moment, Sons of Night wasn't interested in neither the condition of the jogging path nor exercising.

According to their plans, the trio headed to the road cut. Matty felt it was best to follow the jogging path all the way to the farthest bend and then continue straight through the forest to the top of the cliff. Toby thought, though, that Matty was just trying to get him exercise without noticing. Matty said such a thing didn't even cross his mind. Marc, in turn, said he thought the heat had melted his brother's brain but came to the conclusion that the melting had happened already earlier. However, despite Toby's and Marc's teasing, the trio followed Matty's plan.

The hum of the traffic could be heard to the farthest bend of the jogging path. The boys continued walking, Matty in front, through the forest towards the sound. The crown of the hill was a little further from the road cut, so in order to see down to the highway, the boys didn't need to go to the open cliff top. The trio decided then to stay safely behind the tree line.

"That looks like an excellent spot for monitoring," Matty pointed a large spruce which had fallen sideways down the slope. "It's an awesome view from here down the highway."

"Yep, I think this is a good spot," Toby agreed. "We can see the traffic but they can't see us."

Marc noted that the cars heading towards the city couldn't be seen very well. Toby replied they were more interested about the cars coming to Fort

Sara, anyway, so it didn't matter. Matty thought, though, that Marc could be able to see them with his binoculars. The boys put their sleeping pads behind the trunk of the spruce and tried to get a comfortable position on the slope. Marc put his own pad a little higher up the slope in order to see the other lane better.

"Should we write down the license plate number if the van happens to go past?" Marc asked, adjusting the binoculars and focusing on the highway. "Because I can see the plates easily too."

"Well, that doesn't help us much at this stage," Toby replied. "Willie hadn't seen it, if you remember."

Marc wondered what would they do if they happened to see matching red, old and rusty Ford Transit on the move. Toby replied that if it turned towards the town, they would go after it like a flash. Matty doubted the plan and said it was a dud. He didn't believe Toby could go like a flash even after a table loaded with goodies. Toby praised himself and said he was surprisingly fast cyclist when needed but Matty said he wouldn't believe until he saw.

Sons of Night's strategy remained somewhat unclear but the boys started monitoring the vehicles anyway. For a while, the conversation quieted down and each of the trio focused intensively on following the traffic down on the highway. Marc watched with his compact binoculars, Toby and Matty with bare eyes. In the middle of the day, and being weekday, there were few cars on the road. However, there were that much traffic that the boys' didn't lose interest in the job immediately. Mostly there were passenger cars passing by, vans occasionally and infrequently trucks and other heavy vehicles. While observing the traffic, the boys chatted about different car brands and their superiority. And everyone had, of course, their own opinion on the subject.

After twenty minutes of monitoring, Toby was the first to show signs of getting tired. He complained that there were no vans moving on the road, especially not red ones, not to mention Ford Transits. On top of that, he said he was starving. Matty thought that Toby's hunger was in no way surprising.

"Hey, there was a Transit but it was white," announced Matty, gazing firmly towards the highway.

"Bullshit, that wasn't a Transit," Toby snorted. "It was a Transporter, Volkswagen Transporter."

Matty claimed that Toby wasn't even watching when the van passed by.

"It was a Transit alright, Ford Transit," Matty imitated Toby's cocky tone of voice.

Toby replied that even Matty's grandma would have seen it was a Transporter. Matty noted that his granny had, indeed, so poor eyesight that Transit might look like Transporter. Marc listened, amused, to the duo's squabbling. Toby looked questioningly at Marc and wanted to know whether Marc had seen the Transporter.

"You mean the Transit," Matty corrected with a smirk.

Marc said he had watched only the traffic on the other lane.

"But what does it matter anyway?" Marc laughed. "It wasn't red, you know."

"Well, I guess nothing then," Toby muttered, chagrined, realizing the futility of the argument.

Toby announced that he didn't feel like monitoring anymore because the van wouldn't come anyway. Matty pointed out that the traffic monitoring was Toby's idea so he should quit whining. Toby didn't comment anything on that but began to rummage his backpack.

"Don't know about you guys but I'll eat my lunch now."

"Well, that is something you are good at," Matty blurted, realizing immediately that he had gone too far.

Curse words echoed in the woods as Toby got angry and eventually threw Matty with a meat pie package which he had took from the backpack. Luckily for him, Matty had been expecting the shot and managed to catch the package before it would have smacked directly in his face. He handed the package back to Toby and apologized for his words. Matty explained he had just been so annoyed by that arguing about the vans and Toby's cocky behaviour. Marc acted as a conciliator in the dispute and ordered the boys to shake their hands. As the members of Sons of Night, Marc reminded, they should pull together, not fight. Both Toby and Matty agreed it was stupid to argue about such things and shook hands as a symbol of friendship.

The brothers decided also to have a look at what they had for lunch in their backpacks. Matty began to swill juice greedily in large gulps and leaned against the trunk, looking exhausted. He said he was about ready to quit the monitoring because the weather was so damn hot. Toby, who had dragged himself into the shadow away from the blazing sun, replied that he was also ready to go for a swim already.

"There's one thing I don't get," Toby said, glancing at Marc. "How can anyone play football in the heat like this?"

Marc claimed that you didn't even notice the weather while playing. In his mind, football was fun in any weather. Marc admitted, though, that swimming would have been awesome too.

Toby offered his meat pies to the brothers so that they wouldn't spoil in the heat. He gave one even to Matty, although he recalled that he had tried to offer the whole package to him just a moment ago but Matty had rejected it then. Matty chuckled at Toby's joking and said he was now okay with just one pie. However, his half-litre bottle of soda Toby was going to drink himself. He said he needed all of it to replace the lost drops of sweat. Matty and Marc understood it very well.

Unfortunately, Sons of Night lost its focus on the task at hand at a critical moment. The trio was already packing their backpacks and preparing to leave when red, old and rusty Ford Transit was approaching from the direction of the city. The van passed the road cut right under the boys' noses and its blinker went on, signalling that it was about to turn. It was turning to Fort Sara! If Sons of Night had been alert, they would have noticed there were two men in the van. And if Marc had still been watching with his binoculars, he could have seen the co-driver leaning on the side window, just like Willie had seen on the day before. Marc could have seen also the huge skull tattoo on the man's muscular arm.

But Sons of Night wasn't awake. This time.

EIGHT

McBain startled awake from a nap he had fallen into during the trip. The van slowed down and the sound of the blinker shook the last remnants of sleep from McBain's mind. He lifted his sunglasses and glanced at Carter who was driving.

"Are we already there?"

"Fucking moron!" Carter retorted. "We drove here already yesterday and it took only half an hour then. Oh, but you were sleeping the whole trip even then, so how could you know."

Carter was tired and in a bad mood. The previous night's robbery hadn't gone according to plan because McBain's advance information from the target had proven to be false. The plunder had been too small in relation to the risks. In addition, Carter had slept only a few minutes during the last twenty-four hours.

"Calm down! There's no need to lose your rag!" McBain leaned sideways against the window and rolled it down slightly. A blast of cool air rushed inside, tangling McBain's blonde, shoulder-length hair.

Swaying, the old Ford Transit turned from the highway, entering the urban area of Fort Sara. McBain was holding on to the grab handle in order to maintain his balance. He dug his pockets for cigarettes but couldn't find them. Having noticed the gas station Ace One, McBain waved in that direction and told Carter to drive there.

"I've run out of cigarettes. I'll go and buy some."

Carter parked the van in the shadow of the station building, hidden from the scorching sun and away from the staring and prying eyes looking out of the windows. McBain said he would be gone only a moment but Carter decided to turn off the engine anyway. The old van's engine tend to heat up when idling. The tired man sighed heavily and rubbed his dark, close-cropped hair.

Why did I have to join him again, Carter thought as he looked over the fields to the direction of the factory. He opened the window and a cooling breeze blew inside the car. Carter looked into the distance for a moment and then closed his eyes. Instead of this, he could be enjoying the summer without the incessant fear of being caught. But no, McBain had yet again managed to persuade him to come along and here he was.

The two had met each other ten years ago in youth prison. They had shared a cell while serving a year's sentence. The young men, in their twenties then, had become friends and kept in touch with each other ever since. At the time, it had been the first sentence for both of them, McBain had been convicted of car burglaries and drunk driving and Carter of two store robberies.

"Did you manage to fall asleep already?" McBain had returned and tossed a pack of blue Belmont cigarettes at Carter's lap. "And one for you, here you go. It'll calm you down a bit. It was blue you used, right?"

The men lit their cigarettes. Carter told he had been thinking about this situation. He would rather be enjoying the summer instead of feeling constantly tensed. McBain said he had thought that Carter was unemployed and in need of money. Carter admitted he was but would rather earn money legally. He complained that it was just so damn hard for him, as a former inmate, to get a regular job. McBain agreed and said he knew it from his own experience. McBain also said that he probably wouldn't be able to live a normal life anymore. Carter didn't say anything on that.

"Anyway, let's hit the road again," McBain commanded and flicked ashes out the window.

Diesel engine started hard as Carter turned the ignition key. The battery is about to die also, Carter thought but didn't dare to complain anymore. He put the cigarette between his lips, turned the van around and drove to the driveway.

The huge logo of Kermia Ltd. and the main gate of the factory could be seen all the way to the gas station. Carter turned the van to Powder Mill Street and then drove straight towards the factory.

McBain looked at the quiet factory area ahead of them. He wondered what was going on in the world, with job losses and stuff. He had heard that when Kermia was shut down, over three hundred people had lost their jobs. He knew a guy who had worked there as a subcontractor. But good for us, McBain laughed, it would be much easier to break into an abandoned factory. Carter didn't comment on that but turned the car left to Lake Goblin Road, which branched away from Powder Mill Street, couple of hundred meters before the main gate. The men had visited there already the night before so the route was familiar for Carter. They had driven around the factory area just to check it out initially.

"This will be a better target than the previous one," McBain tried to cheer up his mate. "There should be only two guarding rounds per day and video surveillance at the main gate only."

"Well, should be," muttered Carter, the cigarette wobbling between his lips. "There wasn't supposed to be any alarms in the previous target either, but there was anyway."

"But this tip came from another guy," McBain remained optimistic. "The same who had worked at the factory himself.

Carter complained that it was easy for McBain, who could just sit or sleep, while he himself was always driving. McBain didn't have a valid driver's license because of his convictions so Carter was forced to drive. McBain boasted that after this robbery, Carter could afford to sleep in a hotel if he liked.

"We'll just carry the stuff in the van and get the hell out of here. Simple as that."

Transit was bouncing on the bumpy gravel road as Carter was stepping on the gas pedal.

"Maybe I should be driving on these little side roads, after all, because you are driving like maniac," McBain scolded. "Yesterday you almost ran over that biker guy."

"We were in a hurry, thanks to the schedule of yours!"

The planning of the robberies was McBain's responsibility alone. He had contacted Carter a month ago, after getting out of prison yet again. Carter, instead, had tried to live normal life after his first conviction. However, McBain had managed to draw his old mate back to the world of crime.

"Well, thanks to my plan, you don't need any social services or stuff like that anymore."

McBain took the last puff from his cigarette and threw the smoldering butt out of the window.

"You'll burn the whole place down," Carter scolded. "Dry pine forest can catch fire like gasoline in this weather."

The old van continued its bumpy journey, hitting the potholes made by heavy rains earlier in the spring. McBain thought that Carter should focus more on driving than complaining. It seemed to him like Carter was almost aiming at those potholes. At the very moment, Transit once again hit one of those huge holes. At first, a dull thud was heard from the rear, then continuous sound of metal screeching against the road surface.

"God dammit!" Carter cursed and stopped the car at the side of the road. "I guess the exhaust pipe fell off."

The men jumped out of the car to find out what had happened. Carter went down on all fours and peeked under the van. He informed McBain that the exhaust pipe had almost snapped off in front of the middle muffler. McBain replied it wasn't surprising at all because Carter had been aiming at every pothole. Carter, in turn, accused McBain for getting such a piece of crap of a van. He thought that a proper car could handle small bumps without any problems. McBain didn't feel like arguing anymore. He pointed at a small sand mine on the other side of the road and told Carter to drive the van over there.

"Let's fix the pipe temporarily now," McBain instructed. "With cable ties or something. But not here on the road, it would draw too much attention."

Carter did what was told and drove the van, with a terrible screeching sound, to the sand mine.

"You can't crawl under there," Carter complained. "It must be lifted a little bit but we don't have a jack."

"Well, let's just rip the pipe off completely, so we can continue our task."

McBain glanced at his watch and said it would take some time to explore the area. They needed to search a place where they could break inside the factory area, unnoticed. Carter said he had understood that McBain had good information about the area already. About the stuff and the security system he had yes, but not the area itself, McBain declared.

The duo peeked together under the van and tried to loose the exhaust pipe completely. Of the two men, Carter was the taller, almost one hundred and ninety centimeters, McBain fifteen centimeters shorter. Carter could barely reach the pipe and began to shake it back and forth. McBain assisted by waving the pipe from the rear end. After a moment of resistance, the rusted metal gave way and the pipe came crashing down on the ground. Quickly, the men threw the pipe to the trunk of the van and rushed on their way.

Almost two-thirds shortened exhaust pipe was droning loudly as the men drove back on the road.

"So much for that invisibility," Carter had to raise his voice over the noise.

"Well, I'm sure no one is listening at night," McBain soothed. "Let's try to fix the pipe later anyway, though."

Between the trees, on the right side of the Lake Goblin Road, could be seen a chain-link fence which surrounded the factory area. The service road ran beside the fence. The men were now driving in the opposite direction than the day before. Nevertheless, Carter knew where to turn right, to the the road which joined the service road of the factory. It was the same junction where he had almost run over the motorcyclist. At the moment, however, the whole area seemed quiet in terms of traffic.

Carter slowed down as they reached the service road and the fence. McBain wanted to go around the factory area slowly and view it closely. On the other side of the road, stood a sharp embankment. McBain reckoned it was an old railway embankment. The men also saw a road turning left which cut the railway embankment. Bathe Road, Carter read from the road sign, wiping sweat from his forehead. He sighed that a little bathe would be nice alright. However, McBain told Carter to focus only on driving and the factory area on the right.

On the right side, the fence turned away from the road and came back beside the road some thirty meters away. At the end of this recess, the men could see a gate and behind the gate they could see some kind of a rail yard. McBain reckoned the factory had had own railway and yard sometime back in the day. This recess could be a good place to break into the area, McBain thought. Anyway, he told Carter to drive further in case they would find even a better place.

The men kept on driving slowly forward, eyeing the area, until they reached the end of the road. Carter turned the car around. Here and there in the fenced area could be seen small groups of trees and the distances between the buildings were long. There was also many embankments between the different departments. And this all was for the safety reasons. The factory had manufactured explosives so it had been important to prepare for a possible accident. However, at that moment, the duo wasn't interested in the infrastructure of the factory. McBain thought that the gate to the rail yard was the the best place to do the break in. Carter agreed. The men decided to go and take a closer look at the place.

Transit's gearbox crunched as Carter changed gear before turning off the service road towards the rail yard. The men were happy noticing that the van moved effortlessly along the old track. Later they would be pulling a heavy trailer, so without it, the van was supposed to move easily.

"This place looks perfect!" McBain enthused as the men reached the gate.

Carter turned off the van and the men jumped out to look around more closely. McBain grabbed also binoculars from the glove compartment. The men noticed the warehouses at the other end of the rail yard.

According to McBain's source, the stuff was in those warehouses and there should be enough of it to fill the van and the trailer.

"It seems that we can drive all the way to those buildings," McBain reported as he watched the area with his binoculars. "The stuff will be loaded in no time. As easy as taking candy from a baby!"

Carter, who had lit another cigarette, didn't bother to comment anything. He recalled hearing those same words from McBain's mouth before.

McBain had stopped watching with binoculars and was now looking the gate and its lock. He pushed the doors back and forth and said the gate was so lightweight they could drive through it. However, McBain thought it would be better to cut the chain with bolt cutters.

Carter agreed with that, the going would be much quieter that way. But rather than passing the gate, Carter was more worried about the guarding and wanted to know more about that. McBain said they would come to check tonight if the information he had gotten was exact. The tip man had told the guard would do his round twice, in the middle of the night and in the morning.

"Ok, now we're ready, let's go," McBain decided and jumped into the van.

Are we? Carter thought as he stamped his cigarette out. Yet another night of staying awake was coming. He glanced at the yard once more and felt somehow uncomfortable. Like someone was watching.

NINE

There was no single cloud in the sky as Matty and Toby turned from Rocky Hill Street to Powder Mill Street, which ran through open fields. The sun was still shining almost from its zenith and the air above the fields was flickering with heat. Marc had gone straight home from Rocky Hill and the older boys had headed to Lake Goblin for a swim.

The wind blowing from the direction of the factory made pedaling harder but, at the same time, was cooling the air feeling on the skin. The grass growing on the fields was waving in the wind and looked like a green sea. Toby already thought he was so messed up by the heat that saw water everywhere. The boys also noticed a thick dust cloud rising into the air on Lake Goblin road. They supposed there was some vehicle driving along the road but couldn't see it.

The wind had blown the dust cloud away already as the boys turned to Lake Goblin Road. From the open field the road continued into tall pine woods and then turned sharply to the right, reaching soon the fence of the factory area. The boys had to zigzag in order to avoid hitting the numerous potholes in the road. Matty noticed weak dragging marks on the road, which seemed to turn to the old sand mine, but didn't pay them much attention. Toby, in turn, felt so hot that he saw only a vision of a refreshing swim in his mind.

As the boys arrived to the road leading to the service road, Toby told Matty to stop.

"I think it was this junction where Willie was about to collide with that van," Toby said, looking around. "There's a Give Way sign alright, so the van should have stopped and give way to Willie."

Matty wondered what they had been doing there. There was only the service road and the swimming beach in that direction. There were a few summer cottages at Lake Goblin but they were on the other side of the lake. Matty was confident that the men weren't locals because the locals knew there was a Give Way sign in that junction.

"What if they were cottage thieves looking for suitable targets," Toby suggested. "Last winter, there was at least one break-in."

Matty recalled that it had been just some tramp looking for a warm place to stay. Toby didn't remember it exactly any more so he didn't bother to disagree. He complained he was too tired to be able to solve mysteries in this heat, anyway.

The boys carried on towards Lake Goblin. The fenced factory area was on their right, and on the left, the old railway embankment curved near the service road. Matty asked Toby about the embankment. Toby's grandfather had worked in the factory and had told stories about its history. Toby knew that a railroad had once run to the factory but it was closed already years ago.

At its height, the top of the embankment was almost two meters above the boys' heads. At the junction of Bathe Road, there was a narrow opening in the embankment through which the road passed to the other side, continuing towards Lake Goblin and the swimming beach. The wooden bridge, which had once crossed the opening, had rotten and collapsed.

As the boys got to the other side of the embankment, they saw the lake glistening nicely through the tall pine trees. Toby thought it was, at that moment, the world's best scene and Matty could agree with that. The beads of sweat dripping down their foreheads, the duo pedaled the final meters to the shore. It wasn't an official swimming beach but it was very popular amongst the locals. Lake Goblin was known of its velvety sand and clear water. At the moment, however, the boys were interested only in the temperature of the water.

Matty took off his shoes and went to dip his toes in the water.

"Soon we won't be sweating anymore!" Matty informed Toby, who had already put his swimming trunks on.

Toby laughed and said that soon they would be shaking. This was the first swimming trip of the summer for both of them.

"Let's go quickly, then it won't feel so cold," Toby instructed as Matty was also getting ready for the swim.

The boys ran into the water and dived. Matty jumped out of the water almost immediately and gasped.

"This is ice cold!"

Toby couldn't stay in the water much longer so the boys waded to the beach to warm up. Toby guessed that diving was out of the question, even if they got used to the coldness. The boys threw themselves on the warm sand and tried to recover from the ice cold dipping. Matty felt bad they wouldn't be able to explore the bottom of the lake. Toby thought that Willie had fooled them about the water temperature on purpose. Matty chuckled that Sons of Night should take revenge on him one way or another.

Somewhere in the distance, the hum of an engine grew louder but, while chatting, the duo didn't pay much attention to it. Toby told he had heard a rumour at school that some gunpowder had been stored in the middle of the lake.

Apparently, it was from the factory. The story told that some older boys had dived there. Matty said he had heard the same story. He had even seen some of those gunpowder sheets himself, so probably the rumour was true.

The sun was still shining in a cloudless sky and, little by little, the boys began to warm up after the cold dip. Toby squinted his eyes and looked towards the factory. Suddenly, he remembered an interesting story he had heard from his Grandpa. According to Grandpa, some Russian aircraft had crashed inside the factory area. Matty said he had never heard of such an incident before. Toby recalled that it had happened during the war. The aircraft had been bombing the factory when it was shot down. Matty was inspired by the story and urged Toby to tell more. Grandpa had told that the aircraft had crashed somewhere near the rail yard of the factory and that a monument or something should be standing at the crash site. That was all Toby knew about it.

"Let's find the place right away!" Matty enthused.

"But it's inside the fenced area," Toby calmed his friend's enthusiasm. "You can't just go there. Well, you can, but it's not allowed, I think."

The boys considered the matter for a moment. In Matty's view, it wouldn't be so bad thing if they went in there. The factory was closed down anyway. Toby agreed with that but he had concerns about guarding, there could be security cameras like at school.

"Well, why would they keep on monitoring an abandoned factory?" Matty asked. "The place has been closed for years."

Although there wouldn't be any cameras, Toby reminded, they still had to get inside the area somehow. The fence was more than two meters high, it was impossible to climb over it. Matty wasn't worried about such things, he just wanted to search the monument immediately. They could come to swim again later in the summer.

"But how do we find the site?" Matty woke up to reality. "The area is huge!"

"Well, Grandpa told that the plane crashed near the rail yard, more precisely, between the fence and the yard. It's not so large area, probably."

"But how do we find the rail yard?" Matty asked before thought better of it.

"How do you think, Einstein!" Toby ragged.

"Could we find it, perhaps, at the end of that embankment which we passed on the way," Toby said, pointing the railway embankment that could be seen at the end of the lake.

Looking embarrassed, Matty admitted the rail yard could, indeed, be found there. Toby added, jokingly that they just had to know which way to turn. Matty laughed, saying that even he could deduce that.

The boys decided to hide their bikes and backpacks in the woods and walk to the rail yard. By foot, they could take a shortcut along the shore because the railway was only a couple of hundred meters away. The railway had once run right beside the shore and had then turned gradually towards the factory. At the end of the lake, a narrow, clear stream was flowing towards the factory, passing underneath the embankment through an old stone culvert. On the way, Toby and Matty stopped for a moment to watch the stream rippling through the culvert. For Toby, the running water looked invitingly cool and clear. Matty pondered, though, that the water wasn't drinkable, you could get a vole fever or something by drinking it. The boys admired the old culvert and thought it was so big they could go through it if they walked stooped. Pleasantly cool air flooded from inside the culvert and made the boys shiver. Toby would have enjoyed the coolness even longer but Matty was eager to carry on searching the crash site.

The duo climbed up the steep, bushy bank to the top of the embankment and turned towards the factory. The rails and the ties had been removed but the rough gravel surface revealed that there had once been a railway. Nature was slowly taking over the area that had once been taken away from it.

Here and there small pine trees were growing up happily between the crushed stones and a dense willow thicket was growing on both sides of the embankment. The track was bending to the right and descending a little before reaching the service road and the fence of the factory. The boys became vigilant and slowed down their pace as they saw the service road beyond the curve. Matty cursed the loud crunching sound, caused by stepping on the gravel.

The boys stopped to listen and watch the surrounding area before crossing the service road. The track crossed the service road perpendicularly and continued on the other side of the road on par with the ground. The boys already saw the fence and the gate and also the small rail yard behind the gate.

"Ok, there it is then," Toby whispered in a low voice. "Let's sneak behind that gate to see if we could get in somehow."

Matty nodded, tensed. Hunched over, the boys scampered across the service road. Fortunately for them, there wasn't any gravel on the track anymore so the passage became almost silent. The final meters before the gate, the boys crept very quietly, ready to run if something unexpected would happen. However, nothing happened, and there wasn't any movement in the fenced area.

Behind the fence, the rail yard seemed quiet and deserted. The trains had once run into the yard through a double-door gate, which now seemed to be locked. Matty began to have second thoughts and murmured to Toby that maybe this wasn't such a good idea, after all. It would be criminal to trespass into a closed area. Toby, in turn, thought it wasn't such a big deal.

"After all, we won't be breaking anything," Toby tried to justify. "We'll just go in, search the crash site and come back, that's all."

Toby yet added that the factory had been closed for years already. Still, Matty wasn't fully convinced by his friend's arguments but wanted to know how they possibly could break into the area without breaking anything.

Toby began to eye the gate more closely and discovered that it was locked with a heavy-duty chain and a padlock. He pulled the chain and noted that it had been left loose. In Toby's view, it could be possible to pull the doors apart enough so that they could slip through between the doors. They needed just some kind of a tool to wrench the doors apart. Toby looked around and spotted a pile of boards beside the track. The boys reckoned that there had been some sort of a gatekeeper's lodge, which had collapsed. Toby asked Matty to bring one, long board from the pile. Matty did as was told and dug about two meters long board from the pile and gave it to Toby. Toby thought the board was okay even though there were some nails sticking out of it.

The metallic chain-link fence rattled loudly as Toby placed the board between the doors and tried to wrench them apart. Matty cursed the noise in his mind and kept all eyes on the rail yard, ready to flee. Still, no one showed up. The whole area was dead silent.

"Try to go through now," Toby urged Matty.

He was wrenching the gate and managed to get a couple of tens of centimeters gap between the doors. And indeed, Matty managed to crawl to the other side of the gate quite easily. Toby praised Matty's performance but said also that it had to be easy for a skinny guy like Matty.

"Let's see what happens to me."

Toby pushed the board under the gate to Matty who, in turn, began to pry the doors apart. Toby had much more difficulties to weave himself through the opening even though Matty was wrenching as hard as he could to make the gap wider. Matty warned Toby about the nails on the board as Toby was wiggling himself through the gate. Finally, after terrible rattling, panting and wheezing, Toby managed to drag himself to the other side. The boys stayed put and looked around for a while if the noise had caused any reaction, but it was all quiet everywhere.

Exhausted by the effort, Toby was breathing heavily on all fours. Matty chuckled at Toby's wriggling between the doors. He was confident that Toby wouldn't have fit through if he had eaten all the meat pies by himself. Toby admitted the gap had been quite tight. He, again, considered starting a diet because he feared he would otherwise soon miss all the exciting adventures.

Having got through the gate, the boys looked more closely around the yard and the buildings around it. It wasn't actually a proper rail yard, in the truest sense of the word, because there had been only two separate tracks and unloading docks beside them. The rails were gone but the concrete docks were still standing. Behind the rail yard, a little further, was a big warehouse and smaller metal sheds. Small pines and birches grew here and there in an otherwise open area. Toby pointed at a small woods on the left side of the yard, saying he thought that Grandpa had meant that area. Staying low, the duo began to run along the edge of the rail yard towards the woods.

Reaching the edge of the woods safely, the boys sighed with relief.

"I was afraid that a guard or something would jump from behind those sheds at any second," huffed Toby, out of breath.

"Same here!" Matty replied. "Though, there's probably no one here."

However, Toby thought they should still be vigilant and keep noise to a minimum.

Both fortunately and unfortunately for the boys, the forest consisted of densely growing, about three meters tall pine trees. It gave them complete cover but, at the same time, made the search of the crash site more difficult.

"Let's walk up to the fence first so we can see how big this area is," Toby suggested.

They headed deeper into the woods towards the fence which bordered the area. The boys could see one side of the fence on their left, which led them in the right direction. After a while, the other side of the fence began to loom through the trees. Toby asked Matty how long, in his view, was the distance between the rail yard and the fence. Matty estimated it was about hundred meters to which Toby nodded approvingly. Then Toby estimated himself that the rail yard was also about a hundred meters long and began to calculate the size of the area.

"So, if the crash site is between the rail yard and that fence, the search area is a hundred times a hundred meters then. What does it make?"

"You're the Einstein, so calculate yourself!" Matty wasn't interested in doing maths over the summer vacation.

Toby calculated in his mind that it would make ten thousand square meters, which was equal to a hundred ares, which, again, was the same as one hectare. Matty got bored and said that it was pretty well calculated but there was no point. In his view, that information was useless to them.

"How big is a hectare, is it big or small?" Matty asked sarcastically. "You can see it on the ground, you know. You don't need any figures to it."

"I guess so," Toby replied. "But it's good to know how to calculate it also."

Matty began to lose his temper with Toby's engineer-like calculations and said they should begin to search for the site already. He suggested they would walk along the fence, separately. The visibility in the woods was about ten meters so they would get about twenty meters combed at once. Toby rolled his head at Matty's calculations and said he had fucked up. Toby calculated himself that if the both of them saw ten meters in both directions, it would make a total of forty meters then. Matty lost his temper even more even though he agreed Toby was right. He complained that they would have already combed the whole area in the time they had been calculating.

"Okay, let's go and move on," Toby tried to appease Matty. "If you go further away from the fence and I'll search closer."

The boys finally reached some kind of an agreement and began searching the crash site. Matty started to walk back towards the rail yard and walked until he couldn't see Toby anymore. Then he turned to walk parallel with the yard. From time to time, Matty saw a glimpse of the rail yard between the thick pine branches and tried to maintain the right direction. As he reached halfway, he heard Toby's low, wheezing voice from the back left.

"You're not walking straight! Try to stay in line!"

"It's easy for you to say!" Matty snapped back at Toby, complaining that Toby could follow the fence whereas he himself had to walk almost blindly.

Toby pretended not to hear Matty's complaints but told him to turn a bit to the right. Matty grunted and said he would soon turn one hundred and eighty degrees and go home. Toby didn't reply anything on that.

Suddenly, Matty heard a dull thud, followed by muffled cursing from Toby's direction. Toby yelled that he had fallen into some kind of a pit. Matty rushed to find out what had happened.

"Are you okay?" Matty asked as he found Toby lying in a few meters long, shallow depression in the ground.

"Yeah, I'm fine. This trench or something just suddenly came out of nowhere."

While the boys were wondering the depression, noticed Matty about a meter tall stone pillar on the opposite side.

"Hey, that looks like a memorial!" Matty shouted excitedly, jumping past Toby up to the pillar. "So this is where the plane probably crashed!"

Toby crawled out of the trench after Matty and suddenly realized that the impact of the crash had probably caused the depression in the ground. Matty thought the same.

The boys looked at the memorial and wondered what was the long, rusted iron object, attached at the top of the pillar. Matty thought it looked like a propeller blade. Toby went to the other side and noticed a plaque attached to the memorial.

"Yeah, the plane crashed here alright!" announced Toby excited and read out the text engraved on the bronze plaque.

"On this spot on Thursday 26th of June 1941 a russian bomber crashed while it was bombing the factory. Finnish anti-aircraft shot down the bomber and all three crew members were killed. This memorial is erected by Kermia Ltd in cooperation with Citizens Association of Fort Sara."

"How exciting!" Matty got enthusiastic and looked at the depression. "What if the dead were buried here?"

"I don't think so," Toby was lifting his feet as if he feared he was stepping on someone's grave.

Matty laughed and said he was just joking. Toby thought, however, that it wasn't very good subject to joke about.

"But some parts from that bomber could still be found here," Toby said, looking at the ground.

The duo decided to explore the bottom of the depression for a moment. The boys had just jumped into the depression when Matty suddenly stopped to listen.

"Ssh, be quiet!" Matty hissed at Toby. "Listen! A car is coming!"

Now also Toby could hear the sound of an engine coming from behind the fence. The car was driving along the service road. Lightning fast, the boys ducked to the ground and crawled cautiously to the edge of the depression and tried to peek over. The sound grew louder every second and the boys noticed its loud, rumbling tone. They couldn't see much because of the trees but the sound told them enough. The car was almost right in front of them. At that moment, they both saw a glimpse of red between the branches. The boys glanced at each other incredulously. The sound of the engine drifted away.

"It was a red van!" Toby whispered, excited.

"Yes it was," Matty confirmed. "And more than that, I think it was a Transit."

Matty looked at his friend, smiling. Toby nodded, saying he wouldn't start to argue this time, he also thought it had been a Transit.

The sound of the van was still audible.

"What the hell?" Matty turned around towards the rail yard and listened. "It's approaching again!"

To the boys, it sounded like the van was driving along the old railway. Suddenly, the sound ceased entirely. The van had stopped and the engine had been turned off.

"Let's go back and find out what's going on!" Toby lowered his voice again. "But cautiously, we are still trespassing."

The duo headed back to the rail yard. They were moving with caution, trying to avoid stepping on the dead branches lying on the ground. Fortunately, the terrain was mainly a soft moss so it was easy to move silently. The boys flinched as they heard two car door slams from the front. They crept, as low as possible, the last few meters to the edge of the rail yard. There was a low bank between the forest and the yard which gave cover to the boys. They crawled to the bank and peeked over into the rail yard. The red Ford Transit was parked behind the very same gate through which the boys had slipped just moments earlier. Two men were standing in front of the van and were looking towards the buildings in the area.

"What are they up to?" Toby wondered.

"Could they be after us?" Matty frowned, worried.

In Toby's view, the men didn't look like guards, rather suspicious.

The boys had come out of the woods at the far end of the rail yard. The van and the men stood about a hundred meters away from them. Toby cursed the fact they didn't have the binoculars, now it was impossible to see that far. They would have to crawl closer if they wanted to see the license plate number and Toby wanted. Matty wasn't entirely thrilled with the idea but didn't say anything. Keeping as low as possible, the boys crawled on all fours behind the bank, trying to get closer to the gate. Toby went in front and Matty followed reluctantly.

"Don't go any closer!" Matty hissed quietly as Toby just continued crawling forward.

Toby stopped and the duo climbed carefully on the edge of the bank. Now the van and the men stood out clearly. The boys shuddered. The men looked like guys you wouldn't want to run into in a dark alley, or even in the fenced area in daylight. They both looked like they hadn't miss a single meal and had been living in the gym. The shorter of the men had something hanging from his neck. The man took hold of the object and raised it to his eyes.

Binoculars! Matty and Toby realized the situation at the same time and quickly pulled back from the bank.

”Dammit!” Toby hissed. ”It was us who were supposed to have binoculars, not them!”

”Did he see us?” Matty asked in an anguished voice.

”I don't think so,” Toby tried to calm his friend down. ”Did you get the license number?”

Matty shook his head. Toby said he got it himself and thought he would also remember it correctly. Toby took his cell phone from his pocket and wrote the number down. Then he was about to climb back on the bank when Matty suddenly grabbed his shoulder.

”Are you crazy!” Matty whispered. ”We'll get caught because of your curiosity.”

”I'll just peek a little,” Toby replied, lifting his head over the edge of the bank.

Toby informed Matty that the man with the binoculars had finished viewing. He urged Matty to climb back and have a look also. Matty sighed, cursing Toby's curiosity, but dragged himself back on the bank. The blond-haired binocular man had, indeed, finished his watching and was now looking the gate more closely. The taller, short-haired man had lit a cigarette. The binocular man looked at the lock of the gate and then gently pushed the doors a couple of times. The man said something to the cigarette man who nodded in response. The men talked to each other for a while and then seemed to be leaving.

The binocular man turned around to go in the van. At that moment, the boys saw a sight that almost stopped their hearts. The man had a huge tattoo on his muscular arm. It was so huge that there was no doubt about what kind of a tattoo it was. A skull and crossbones!

On the bank, the boys ducked their heads quickly.

"Damn!" Toby looked at Matty with his eyes wide open in amazement. "Did you see that? Those *are* the same guys!"

Matty nodded, looking serious and still tried to suggest that the men were just guards on their rounds. Toby didn't believe that. Those guys didn't look like guards to him, not one bit. Besides, the van they used was just a piece of junk, it didn't look like a security service vehicle. Matty said he just tried to come up with a logical explanation for the men being there. Toby believed the men were doing something fishy and boasted that Sons of Night would find out what it was.

Behind the gate, the Transit's engine was already running and the gearbox crunched as the driver put the gear in reverse. The van backed away and the loud engine sound disappeared in the distance. The boys sighed with relief, laying still for a moment. Matty wondered what could possibly interest the men here, in a closed factory. Toby believed there could still be something valuable in those warehouses, perhaps even explosives. Matty didn't believe that. But something strange was going on for sure, Matty was ready to admit that by now.

"Sons of Night has a case here!" Toby enthused.

"Do you mean that we would come here at night?" Matty asked in surprise. To him, the idea was just absurd.

Toby explained it could be done during the day also. Or, during the following night, when patrolling at the school area, they could also keep an eye on the traffic heading towards the factory.

"Well, how much traffic could possibly be heading in that direction at night?" Matty snorted. "Watching paint dry would be more interesting."

Despite Matty's doubts, Toby said he had a feeling in his bones that something strange would happen at night. Matty replied that he, too, had a feeling but it was in his belly and it also had a name: a hunger. Toby laughed and said he was no stranger to that feeling either.

The sun had gone behind a cloud as the boys sneaked back to the gate. The rail yard looked darker and even more abandoned now. The duo managed to crawl through the doors again and headed back to their bikes.

On the way home, Toby and Matty discussed about the coming night. Toby recommended that the brothers would come to the hut early so they would have time to make detailed plans for the night. The boys decided to take enough warm clothes along because, according to the weather forecasts, it was going to be a cold night. And the balaclavas of course, Toby told Matty to remind Marc also about that. The duo pondered whether to tell Willie about the Transit or not. However, Toby thought it was better not to tell. Sons of Night would handle the case alone.

TEN

"Why on earth do you need knit caps in summer?" Matty's and Marc's Mom asked in amazement when the brothers asked for old caps. "And why they have to be black?"

Matty mumbled something about Cops and Robbers game.

"And if we could cut them a little," added Marc timidly. "Holes for eyes and mouth."

The boys were sure that the answer would be strong no.

"Oh, so you are going to turn them into balaclavas."

The brothers looked at each other, smiling. Sometimes Mom surprised them for sure.

"Exactly!"

Fortunately, Mom didn't ask any more questions but told that the old knit caps were in a cardboard box in the storage room. She asked the boys to look over there themselves. Satisfied, the duo walked to the storage room. After a little searching, they managed to find the right box and started to look through the caps for suitable ones.

Marc hadn't yet heard about Matty's and Toby's adventures at the factory. He had come from the football practice just a while ago and, because of Mom's presence, Matty hadn't had a chance to tell him about the events. In the storage room, Matty told what had happened at the rail yard and Marc listened in amazement. At first, Marc thought Matty had made up the whole story but then came to the conclusion that even Matty couldn't come up with such a crazy incidents. Marc began to feel disappointed that he hadn't gone with the two. However, Matty comforted his brother, saying that Marc would surely get enough adventure tonight.

The boys could find only one black cap but Matty thought the dark blue one they did find would do. The brothers decided they would cut the holes later on at the hut. Toby's balaclava could be used as a model.

"Did you find suitable?" Mom had appeared at the storage room door.

The boys showed the knit caps they had found and Mom nodded approvingly. In her view, the caps looked old and ragged enough to be cut, nobody would use them anymore anyway. Mom began to ask questions about the night in the hut and reminded the boys that they should also take warm clothing along, other than balaclavas. Matty and Marc promised to do so, adding that everything was well planned and under control and that they were just about to go upstairs to pack their backpacks. The boys realized that Mom was getting in her caring mode, so it was better to leave the scene.

The brothers' home was an old, wooden, two-storey house, which was located on Stonebridre Road, in a quiet neighbourhood on the south side of Fort Sara. The boys had their own rooms upstairs where, besides the rooms, was just a narrow corridor leading to the rooms. For that reason, the whole upper floor was their kingdom, or at least the boys wanted to think so.

Upon reaching the upper floor and escaping their Mom's fussing, the boys started to pack up the necessary gears for the night. Following Toby's instructions, they packed dark outerwear and flashlights. Marc also took his binoculars. The boys shilly-shallied between the warm clothes, what to take and what to leave. Marc was going to take the long johns but Matty thought it would be too much, it was summer, after all. Matty began to tease Marc about his action talks again. He laughed that no action hero would never ever wear long johns.

"Well, let's see who's laughing at night," Marc snapped. "You'll have poop in your pants and cold too."

"Who will have poop in one's pants and why?" Mom had come upstairs and was standing at the door.

"Nobody," Matty hurried to reply. "I was just teasing Marc a little, you know, that he's gonna miss Mommy at night."

Mom laughed and said that there was nothing to be ashamed of. It would be just nice if one of the two still missed her sometimes. Mom reminded the boys about the visit to Aunt Helen at the following day. She told them to come home not later than half eleven, preferably even earlier. The boys assured they would come on time. The visit to Aunt Helen had been agreed before the boys knew they were going to spend the night at the hut.

The boys got their gear packed up. Mom didn't ask about their equipments any more but said that supper was ready, no one would go anywhere without eating first. Obediently, the boys went for a supper although Marc complained he wasn't hungry. After having some yogurt and sandwiches, the boys were finally able to leave. They felt as if Mom had gone through all possible warnings in the world before letting them go.

The evening sun cast its last rays into the woods as the boys arrived to the hut. Both Matty and Marc began to feel a small tingle of excitement in their stomach. Toby was sitting in the doorway of the hut and wished the boys welcome at the Sons of Night headquarters. He suggested they should immediately start a meeting, regarding the forthcoming night. Matty wanted to know if Toby was going to act as a chairman again and speak formally. Toby replied that he was just one of the members of Sons of Night, not a chairman. Matty said he had nothing against planning but any formal nonsense he didn't want to hear. Toby promised to speak and behave normally.

All three climbed upstairs and laid down on the mattresses. Toby opened the conversation about the night ahead. He said he had already thought about the route to the school before and was of the opinion that they should take the bicycles to the side of the road beforehand.

"Are we going by bicycles?" Marc asked in amazement. "I thought we would go by foot."

In Toby's view, it would be wiser to go by bicycles because the school was almost a kilometer away and, perhaps, they would patrol elsewhere too. Matty agreed with Toby but Marc wondered how they would manage to ride in the dark. The two thought, however, that it wouldn't be a problem.

"So we'll walk along the path to Meadow Street and then take the bicycles, which we have carried there beforehand," Toby pulled together the plan and explained the route to the school which he thought was the best.

Both the brothers thought it sounded like a good route. Then, the boys pondered the best place for monitoring and everyone agreed that the small woods next to the school yard would be the best option. They knew the area well and it offered good cover for them.

"Okay, that's all, I think," Toby looked at the brothers questioningly. "We'll improvise the rest along the way, right?"

Neither Matty nor Marc had anything to add or any questions, so the boys went out to take their bikes on the roadside. After returning back to the hut, the trio decided to try to sleep a bit before leaving. Toby reckoned that, because of the brightness, they could leave no earlier than eleven pm. And secondly, there wouldn't probably be much going on before the sunset, anyway.

"Shit!" Marc suddenly cursed when the boys had just crawled into their sleeping bags. "We forgot to make the balaclavas!"

The boys couldn't help but to get up and start working. Toby showed his balaclava and the brothers tried to copy the model. Toby thought it didn't have to be so precise because you could stretch the fabric and adjust the holes while wearing the balaclava. Matty laughed at Marc's balaclava when the boys were trying on their creations. Marc had left the tassel hanging on the top of the cap and Matty thought it destroyed their street credibility. However, Marc let the tassel be because, in his view, it fitted well with their gang's image. Toby chuckled and agreed that they were more soft than tough.

After crafting the balaclavas, the trio tried to have some sleep again. But soon, Toby and Matty began to think back to the incidents at the factory and Marc listened, annoyed, to the conversation having missed the exciting trip. Toby and Matty comforted him, however, saying that he would certainly get enough excitement at night. Matty confessed that he had been pretty scared seeing the men closer. Those guys had looked somehow creepy. Toby agreed and said that the word "criminal" was almost written on their foreheads. The boys couldn't come up with any good reason for the men being there. Not that they had done anything illegal but their behaviour had been strange anyway. Matty chuckled that he and Toby had also been there, and even inside the fenced area, so it was early to judge those guys.

Gradually, the boys' chatting quieted down as the sleep caught up with them one by one.

"I put the alarm at 11.30 pm," Toby yet mumbled. "It should be dark by then."

"Mm-m," a muffled response was heard from the depths of the sleeping bags.

Soon, a steady breathing filled the silence of the night.

ELEVEN

Marc woke up, startled, and for a moment didn't realize where he was. He felt the coolness of the early night on his face. It was almost pitch dark in the hut. Marc glanced at his cell phone, the clock showed 11.15 pm. The two other members of S.O.N seemed to sleep soundly. Suddenly, Marc froze to listen. He heard a rustling sound coming outside. Frightened, Marc shook his older brother whose legs happened to be conveniently within reach.

"Matty! Wake up!" Marc whispered. "There's someone out there!"

"What?" grunted Matty, still half asleep.

"Listen!"

Matty sat up and tried to listen. He commented wearily that he couldn't hear anything and told Marc to calm down. Toby also woke up to the ruckus caused by the brothers and asked what was it all about. Marc insisted that he had heard something from outside. Matty didn't believe there was anything but thought that Marc had been dreaming. Toby, who had slept closest to the window, tugged the sleeping bag's hood off and ordered both to be quiet. He wanted to listen more closely through the window.

"There's something moving alright!" whispered Toby anxiously, confirming that Marc was right.

Still in his sleeping bag, Toby twisted himself on his knees and took a look through the window. At first, he couldn't see anything in the low light of the night, but then a dark lump moved a few meters away from the hut. Toby burst into relieved laughter.

"Come over here, quickly!"

The brothers wormed their way to the window in their sleeping bags. They barely managed to catch a glimpse of a creature which, apparently scared by the boys' voices, left the scene.

"What on earth was that?" Marc asked in surprise.

"I think it was a raccoon dog," Matty replied and Toby nodded approvingly.

Marc hadn't seen one before, and neither had Matty even though he had recognized it. Toby knew that the raccoon dogs were moving mainly at night.

"Anyway, it really scared me!" Marc sighed.

"Some Sons of Night we are," Toby laughed. "All jumpy before the real action."

Anyhow, the raccoon dog had woken the boys just in time. Sons of Night's first official mission was about to begin.

The air felt uncomfortably cold after being in the warm sleeping bag. The trio hastily put more clothes on. They all had dark clothes as earlier had been agreed. Toby told to put the balaclavas on right away, they would warm nicely. The boys looked at each other with amusement. They thought they looked like criminals themselves, except Marc, who had a tassel hanging on top of his balaclava.

"Now, let's go and prevent some crimes!" Toby declared in a low voice as the boys slapped high fives with each other to boost the spirit.

A cool breeze greeted the members of S.O.N as they stepped outside and, together with the growing excitement, gave them chills. The sky had begun to cloud over and the moon, which had risen above the horizon earlier, was no longer visible. The trio began to sneak along the path which led to Meadow Street. The night was darkening quickly and, in some places, it was already difficult to follow the path. The boys had agreed they wouldn't use flashlights or bicycle lights, expect if necessary, as they would draw too much attention. Fortunately, Toby knew this forest like the back of his hand, and with firm steps, he led the gang over to the bicycles.

For the trio's surprise, the street lights on Meadow Street weren't on. The boys dragged their bicycles to the dark street and noticed that the street lights were off everywhere. Matty reckoned the lights were turned off to save energy because in the summer, the darkness lasted only a few hours. Toby thought the situation was good for them. It was much easier to stay out of people's sight now.

The boys began to ride without lights towards the school. Along Meadow Street to the north, and then to the west along the walkway between detached houses. Here and there could still be seen lights through the windows, but no one seemed to be outside as the midnight was approaching. Toby's route plan was also such that they would avoid the busiest streets and places. The journey continued over Rowan Street and straight ahead down the alley. On the left side of the alley, a dog started barking furiously as Sons of Night hurtled past. The boys were frightened by the sudden ruckus but continued on their way along the path, which went through a park.

"Damn, I almost wet my pants," Toby panted as the boys had gotten further away from the houses. "Didn't remember that O'Malley's dog always bark like that."

"How come it's still outdoors, it's almost midnight?" Matty asked with amazement. Toby reckoned that the dog was always kept outside, except for the coldest nights.

The park, through which the boys were riding, was just a narrow strip of forest and not far from the school. In between, was just a tree-lined street named Borough Street, which passed through Fort Sara. The path ended on the street and the small forest, where the boys were heading, was immediately on the other side. The trio had suggested that crossing Borough Street would be the hardest part of the journey. There could still be traffic on the town's main street. Before the street, the boys got off the saddle and walked the final meters. However, the street was dark and quiet, so the trio rushed across it and continued straight to the forest. They left their bikes behind the nearest trees and continued on foot towards the school.

The small forest next to the school consisted of sparsely growing, tall pine trees and a number of trails, made by pupils, criss-crossed the area. Many nature trips and exercise classes had been held in that forest. So, the boys knew the area thoroughly and, even in the dark, could choose the right paths which led them to the school yard. Closer to the school, the terrain turned more rocky. Therefore, the boys had planned they would monitor the school from behind some suitable sized stone. The school yard was brightly lit and could be seen far away. Toby reckoned that more lighting had been added to prevent vandalism. S.O.N managed to get closer to the yard without problems and anxiously took positions behind about a meter high stone.

The sky had now clouded over completely and the night darkened further. The lights in the school yard formed a ghostly halo in the middle of the darkness. Everywhere seemed quiet. The boys watched the yard in silence and listened carefully for a moment. A muffled sound of traffic could be heard from the town in the distance, but otherwise all was quiet. Marc had dug the binoculars out of his pocket and was watching the school building and the yard more closely.

"It seems that no one's there at the moment," Marc reported. "And all seem to be okay."

Matty began to complain about the cold already and jumped in place to keep warm.

"So, what did you say about the long johns again?" Marc couldn't help needling his brother a bit.

Toby said also that it was Matty's own stupidity, feeling cold already at this point. Matty didn't comment on that but turned the talk back to S.O.N operation. He thought that this lurking thing was pretty pointless. He didn't believe there would be vandalism on two consecutive weekends.

"Yeah, well, let's just wait calmly and see if there's something happening," replied Toby.

The situation annoyed Toby because the idea of the secret society was his own, and now it looked like the first night mission was turning into a total fiasco. It was good, though, that nothing happened but it would be boring to do the patrols without any action.

The minutes passed but the school yard still remained quiet. The darkest moment of the night was approaching and the temperature continued to drop. Matty had started jumping again.

”Who was the idiot who said that long johns aren't necessary?” Matty joked self-ironically. ”Damn, it's cold out here!”

Marc began to laugh and said he felt cold too even though he had long johns on. Toby didn't say anything but his body language told that he was no longer warm either.

”Nothing is going to happen tonight!” Matty complained, looking bored. ”Let's go back already!”

Toby glanced at his cell phone. The time was five past midnight. They had been on the move only a little over half an hour and they all were bored and cold. Toby was embarrassed. He had been so proud about this night patrol idea. And here they were in the middle of the night, the great Sons of Night, staring at the empty school yard and feeling cold.

”Okay, let's go,” Toby said in a dejected voice.

The atmosphere was quiet and grim as the boys shuffled through the dark forest back to where their bikes were. After a short search, they found the bikes and pushed them to the road. As the trio was about to cross Borough Street, a strained roar of the engine coming from the distance suddenly broke the silence. Someone or ones were approaching along the street and fast.

"Back into the woods, quickly!" Toby shouted a warning.

The boys dashed back behind the trees, trying to find some cover. Two lights appeared in the distance and kept coming closer as the engine sound became stronger. After a few seconds, two mopeds roared past at full throttle and headed towards Fort Sara Road.

"The Monkey Twins!" Toby almost spat the words out of his mouth. "Those maniacs rode probably seventy, at least, and the speed limit is forty kilometer per hour!"

The trio scrambled back to the street and saw a glimpse of the Monkey Twins as they turned from Borough Street to Fort Sara Road and headed towards Ace One. The boys made a quick decision to go after the mopeds even though they knew that Zac and Archie were already far away. Toby reminded that those bastards they were actually chasing in the first place, so S.O.N wouldn't give up easily.

Riding in Indian file, the boys went after the Monkey Twins. Toby was driving at the head, Marc second and Matty was watching their back. On the left side of Borough Street, the houses were already dark, except for a few garden lights that had been left on. The boys passed the lighted school yard which no longer aroused any interest in them. Everywhere was quiet, except for the sounds of the mopeds drifting away. The whole town seemed to be sleeping already.

After reaching Fort Sara Road, the boys were able to ride more relaxed because there were fewer houses in that part of the town. The trio reckoned that there could still be some traffic but believed they would have enough time to hide, if necessary. They decided to ride all the way to Ace One and have a look if the Monkey Twins had possibly gone to refuel. The cafe wasn't open at night but there was a pay-at-the-pump system.

However, as the boys reached the gas station, there was no one there. Both the front yard and the gas pump area were empty. They listened silently for a moment but heard nothing. On the highway leading to the city, street lights were burning brightly but there was no movement either.

”Would they be heading all the way to the city?” Toby expressed doubts.

Matty thought it was possible because those tuned mopeds moved almost as fast as a car.

Suddenly, somewhere in the distance, a sound of a warning siren was heard which, however, seemed to be moving further away. An argument broke out among the trio about the source of the alarm sound. Toby was sure that it was an ambulance but Matty claimed the sound belonged to a police car. Marc said it could have been even a fire engine, he wasn't terribly interested in arguing about the matter in the middle of the night. He was cold and his fingers had frozen during the cycling.

As the members of Sons of Night were bickering, a vehicle coming from the direction of the city had reached almost the junction to Fort Sara. The boys didn't wake up to the reality until the car was already signalling to turn.

"A car is coming!" Matty noticed the danger first and yelled a warning. "And it's turning this way!"

In panic, the boys tried to look for a place to hide. Toby noticed a nearby bus stop shelter and roared instructions to the brothers. All three threw their bikes into a ditch and rushed behind the shelter. The car approached the intersection of Fort Sara Road and Powder Mill Street. It almost stopped at the t-junction and its lights swept the shelter, behind which the boys were crouching.

The car turned left to Powder Mill Street towards the factory and Lake Goblin. The boys peeked cautiously from behind the shelter. The car was a van! A sudden feeling of horror seized Toby and Matty when they realized it. The van looked familiar! Toby managed to read the license plate and his facial expression told Matty more than a thousand words. The van was definitely the same they had seen earlier in the day.

Sons of Night's first real mission had began miserably but now it was about to take a thrilling turn!

TWELVE

McBain felt frustrated. He had just finished carrying the previous night's plunder in the cellar. The amount had been even lower than he had expected. McBain sighed heavily and closed the cellar door behind him. A bigger catch would be needed and soon, he wondered as he strode back to the house. He and Carter were staying at an abandoned house which they used as a temporary base while doing their burglaries. The same guy, who had tipped them about Kermia Ltd's warehouses, had recommended the place for McBain. And indeed, its location was almost perfect: suitably isolated but still a short distance from a number of potential burglary sites. And, at least, until this day, no one had disturbed them and the stuff had remained safe in the cellar.

Carter was just crawling from under the Transit as McBain returned to the house.

"Did you get it fixed?" McBain asked.

"The whole pipe should be changed but it will hold a little while now."

Carter looked tired even though he had slept a couple of hours after coming from the factory. McBain told Carter to start the engine. Carter wiped the dirt from his hands on his boiler suit, jumped into the cab and started the van. The sound of the engine was markedly quieter than earlier and McBain praised Carter for good work.

”What about the plunder?” Carter asked, after turning the engine off. ”How big it was?”

”It wasn't,” McBain waved his hand in the air. ”I think we could make only about three grand off it.”

”Well, it's better than nothing.”

That McBain admitted but added immediately that from Kermia, they should get a five times bigger catch. McBain looked at the van and the trailer, standing at the corner of the house, and estimated that together those two could carry three thousand kilos, at least. That amount of stuff would be worth of over fifteen thousand in euros. Carter's expression brightened. He thought that the money was practically handed to them. An abandoned factory and loads of stuff worth thousands, served on a silver platter. McBain, however, told his mate to hold his horses and pointed out that the factory was still guarded. And the stuff had to be sold forward before it would turn into money.

”A few similar heists a year and you don't need to do anything,” Carter was already dreaming. His previous pessimism seemed to be long gone.

McBain burst into laugh.

"I've heard those words probably a thousand times. And yet, both of us have been serving time."

The night had darkened fast and it was already difficult to see around. McBain glanced at his watch. He told Carter to let the van down from the jack and prepare for departure. The tipman had revealed that the factory guard would do his rounds at night between half past midnight and one am. Carter wondered why they had to go there once again if the guard's schedule was already known. McBain explained that they should make sure and know the schedule exactly. Otherwise the guard could be on his rounds just when they were doing the break-in.

After lowering the van down and getting it ready, Carter took off his boiler suit and threw it, and the jack, into the trunk. In his view, the heist could have been done already tonight. However, McBain was in charge and was pulling all the strings. Carter himself was just a mere helper.

The men jumped into the van and drove off towards Fort Sara. It took ten minutes to drive to the highway and then twenty minutes to the factory. As usual, McBain took a comfortable position and announced that he was trying to sleep. Carter reckoned it wouldn't remain just a try. He recalled that McBain had sometimes fallen asleep even during a five-minute drive. McBain told

Carter to be quiet, his recalling disrupted his attempt to sleep.

McBain was already fully asleep when Carter turned the van onto the highway. After driving a while, he noticed a car's headlights approaching from behind. A cold sweat broke out on his forehead as he recognized the vehicle. It was a patrol car!

"McBain!" Carter shouted tensely. "The cops are driving behind us!"

Sleepy McBain didn't understand the situation immediately and Carter had to repeat it. McBain leaned forward and glanced in the side mirror.

"Yeah, so it seems," the situation didn't seem to bother McBain. "So what?"

"Well, what if they pull us over!"

McBain wondered why on earth the police would pull them over. He told Carter to stop panicking. That's why he had unloaded the van of the stuff, so they wouldn't need to worry about the police. The van was okay and they didn't have any warrants so they didn't have anything to worry about. Yet. Twenty-four hours later they would have the van and the trailer full of stolen goods, McBain said, advising Carter to be calm, at least, until then.

Suddenly, blue lights began to flash behind them and, for a moment, even McBain thought the police was going to check them. However, Carter announced that the red stop light wasn't flashing. Indeed, the patrol car overtook their van and sped off. The police wasn't after them. As the patrol car disappeared in the horizon, Carter sighed with relief. He complained that he was allergic to the cops. McBain laughed and said it was a common ailment amongst the felons.

It became silent in the van for a moment as the men fell into thought. McBain's tiredness had disappeared. McBain gave Carter to understand that he was all calm but he wasn't, really. He was thinking about how they had managed to screw up many opportunities even though things had looked good, like now. And the cops weren't stupid, they always seemed to find a way to track them down somehow.

"Got any cigarettes?" Carter's question broke the silence and awakened McBain from his thoughts.

"Yes, I have, have you?" McBain teased. "Did you run out of ciggies again?"

Carter explained that he wasn't out of cigarettes but he had forgotten them in the boiler suit pocket. McBain claimed Carter had done it on purpose so that he could scrounge some. Carter denied such a thought, saying that he would never be so dishonest. McBain burst into spontaneous laughter. In his view, there was a contradiction between Carter's words and deeds. But Carter claimed to be an honest thief. McBain thought about his mate's words for a while and replied that maybe that could be one way to think. Carter asked again for a cigarette but McBain said that Carter was a grown man and could wait until they reached their destination.

"Besides," McBain continued. "You should reduce smoking so you might live longer."

"Well, well, well, look who's talking," snorted Carter. "And it's not easy when your life is nerve-racking like this."

"Well, it has been your own choice!"

An argument developed between the two about how much it depended on oneself how one's life would be. Carter argued that not all have the same chances in life. Some were born with a golden spoon in their mouth and some others were born in a slum. McBain agreed that that was, of course, true but he was of the opinion that one could live right or wrong regardless of one's background. Carter admitted it could be possible but continued to insist that poor upbringing would affect one's later life. McBain wondered would it be impossible to raise a child right in a poor environment. Carter got frustrated and said he didn't feel like arguing anymore because McBain obviously didn't seem to understand his point. McBain replied that it was a discussion, not an argument, but he didn't want to continue either. It became silent in the van again.

It was almost pitch black beyond the street lights. However, the pale glow in the western sky revealed that it hadn't been long ago when the sun had set behind the horizon. Ace One's lighted billboard appeared from behind Rocky Hill and Carter switched the turn signal on. The street lights of Fort Sara weren't burning so, after turning off the highway, Carter switched the high beams on. Ford Transit's bright headlights swept across the darkness, reaching eventually the reflective street signs of Powder Mill Street and Fort Sara Road. Carter was focused on driving and McBain was leaning against the side window, with his eyes closed. The beam of the headlights struck also to the bus shelter on the right side of the t-junction. The men didn't notice the three boys in dark clothes and balaclavas, who had barely managed to hide themselves behind the shelter. But the boys didn't miss the red Ford Transit driving towards the factory.

Sons of Night was on the move!

THIRTEEN

"Come on! Let's go after them!" Toby shouted a command.

Transit's big, red taillights receded in the direction of the factory. The boys snatched their bikes from the ditch and went after the van, pedaling like maniacs.

"Was that the van you saw?" Marc asked as he caught up Toby who was riding in front and panting heavily.

Being out of breath, Toby replied just a short yes. Matty appeared also from behind asking what was their plan. In his view, they shouldn't just rush after the van without having a second thought. Toby slowed down a little so they could talk. He reckoned they could ride safely, at least, until reaching the service road. Those men were presumably heading to the same place as earlier in the day, to the rail yard.

The boys saw the Transit turning onto Lake Goblin Road. It was now moving laterally and its headlights stood out as a narrow stripe in the middle of the field. The mist, which had begun to creep over the field, looked like a white wall in front of the lights. Soon, the boys lost sight of the van, though, as it disappeared into the woods.

In the middle of the field the air felt even cooler. Especially Matty felt the coldness in his bones but didn't care about it at the moment. The trio turned onto Lake Goblin Road and soon found out that riding on it was almost impossible. It was hard to see the bumps and potholes in the dark and the handlebar struck unpleasantly every time the front wheel hit one of those holes. The boys couldn't help but turn the lights on. They counted on Toby's assumption that the men would drive directly to the gate.

Beyond the range of their lights, everything was coal-black but the members of S.O.N didn't feel any fear. At least not yet. The togetherness gave them extra courage. Hardly any of the boys would have come alone at Lake Goblin, in the dark. The trio reached the fork in the road and turned towards the service road. They slowed down a little as they were approaching the factory area. On the left, a familiar embankment stood out as a dark wall and the fence of the factory gleamed on the right.

Suddenly, Toby, who had been riding in front, hit the brakes and turned the light off quickly. Instinctively, the brothers did the same, though they didn't realize the reason for Toby's maneuver.

"What is it?" whispered Matty anxiously.

"There, in that opening!" Toby replied in a low voice. "Something flashed there!"

They were only about twenty meters from the opening, through which Bathe Road passed. However, what ever it was, they couldn't see it in the dark. The boys listened for a moment, quiet as a mouse, but the whole area was completely silent.

"Let's sneak closer," Toby whispered.

"Let's get out of here!" Marc said in a fearful voice, resisting the idea. "We don't know what's in there."

Matty thought that now his brother had shat in his pants, after all, but Marc denied it. Toby said Marc could turn back whenever he wanted. However, Marc wasn't too excited about the idea of returning back to the hut alone, so he decided to stay. Toby praised him being a true Son of Night.

Slowly and carefully, the trio crept closer to the opening. On the right side of the road, stood out a large, box-like object. Toby dug out his flashlight and directed it towards the object. The rear reflectors of the red Ford Transit sparkled brightly as the beam of light hit them.

"Shit!" Toby hissed and urgently turned the flashlight off. "Let's get off the road, quickly!"

The boys retreated rapidly into the woods on the other side of the road and had a short negotiation.

"What is going on?" wondered Matty. "Where are they?"

Toby guessed the men had gone to the rail yard on foot. They had, for some reason, wanted to park their van behind the railway embankment in hiding.

"But what the hell are they doing here at this time?" wondered Marc in turn.

"Well, Sons of Night is going to find that out!" Toby boasted and Matty agreed.

Marc began to protest again but Matty and Toby remained strict. This was why the whole secret society was formed in the first place, and the one who came up with the name S.O.N, shouldn't be the first to back out. The duo had managed to pull the right strings and again Marc agreed to stay with. Matty yet reminded that they would move carefully so nothing bad would happen. The bikes would be left behind, and they would go by foot.

Sons of Night headed on its way. The trio decided to walk along the embankment, instead of the service road. The old railway track passed behind the tree line so they wouldn't be seen from either the road or the factory area. The boys' only concern was the rough gravel on the track which was crunching loudly under their feet. Luckily, there was a narrow strip without the gravel at the edge of the track and the boys tried to walk along it. The branches of the willow trees, growing on the side of the embankment, hit constantly in the face and the boys had to bend them out of their way. In the dark, the going was slow anyway and it took nearly ten minutes for the trio to walk a couple of hundred meters. Toby, who was once again in front, noticed a rippling sound of a stream coming from below and realized that right there he and Matty had climbed up on the bank earlier in the day. However, in the dark, everything looked quite different or, in fact, didn't look anything. There was just blackness everywhere, only the sky looked a little lighter. Finally, the track began to bend back towards the service road and from that the boys knew they were approaching the level crossing and the rail yard behind it.

Abruptly, Toby stopped again so quickly that Marc walked right into him and Matty, who was at the back, collided with Marc.

"Do you smell the same?" Toby asked, whispering and sniffed in the direction of the rail yard. "A smell of cigarette smoke!"

Indeed, now Matty and Marc could also smell it quite clearly. Someone was obviously smoking nearby. Toby urged to proceed even more cautiously, no extra sound was allowed. Meter by meter, the boys crept forward and could already see the service road, being lighter than the rest of the surroundings. Finally, they saw the rail yard behind the road. The outdoor lights were burning at the warehouses in the factory area. On the left side of the track, before the service road, was a dark blob. Toby and Matty had seen it during the day but hadn't paid attention to it then. However, Toby remembered that it was apparently some kind of a grit box.

"Let's crawl behind that grit box," Toby whispered, pointing at the dark blob ahead.

The trio went slowly on all fours behind the grit box. They listened quietly for a moment but nothing was heard. Only a light breeze swished the leaves of the trees. Toby dared to peek over the box first and the brothers followed their friend's example.

There was no movement inside the fenced area. The service road in front of the boys was also dark and quiet. They could still smell the odor of cigarette smoke. At that very moment, all the members of S.O.N stiffened in horror and ducked their heads down behind the grid box.

"Did you see that?" Matty gasped.

Marc and Toby nodded. They all had seen the same chilling sight on the other side of the road, at the edge of the woods. A man's face that had horrendously glimmered in the glow of the cigarette. Both Toby and Matty were sure that the man was the same they had seen there earlier in the day: the tattooed binocular man. Suddenly, a dry cough was heard from the other side of the road, followed by a quiet conversation. The other guy was there too.

"What on earth are they doing?" Matty wondered.

Neither Toby nor Marc had an explanation why the men were standing there in the middle of the night. Matty and Toby decided to try to peek at the men if they could find out more.

Now the boys could see two glowing tips as the men drew on their cigarettes. For a while, their faces stood out in the dark glowing fire-red. The scene was like a horror movie. The boys couldn't understand what the men were waiting for. However, something shady was going on that was for sure. Toby and Matty were so focused on watching the men that didn't notice the lights flashing through the trees. But Marc, who had stayed low behind the box, noticed them instead and nudged the two.

"A car is coming!" Marc warned, whispering.

Matty and Toby ducked down quickly. Now the trio could already hear the sound of the car, it was approaching from the direction of Lake Goblin Road. The car's bright headlights cast ghostly shadows over the trees. The boys tried to make themselves as small as possible, so that not a single part of their bodies would be visible from the road. Then, the car seemed to be slowing down and fear and panic took over Sons of Night. Why it was slowing down? Did the driver spot them? Suddenly, the headlights turned and disappeared. The boys realized the car didn't continue down the service road but turned towards the rail yard.

Curiosity overcame Marc's fear and, like Matty and Toby, he got up to see what was going on. The car had stopped in front of the gate to the rail yard. It was a security patrol car. A guard, wearing uniform, stepped out of the car and walked with a swift pace to the gate. He checked the gate promptly and then returned back to the car. The reverse lights lit up and, again, the boys went down on the ground.

Engine whining, the car backed up fast and for a moment its headlights lightened the area as the guard turned back onto the service road. The patrol car continued on its journey along the service road and was soon lost from sight. After that, the forest was dark and quiet again. In great excitement, the boys waited what would happen next.

Although they didn't here anything at first, the trio was able to sense that the Transit-men were still on the other side of the road. Then the same dry cough was heard again but this time much closer. The men were on the move and heading right towards the boys' hiding place!

The trio was lying behind the grit box, terrified. Marc and Matty were lying face down, only Toby dared to watch from the corner of his eyes. The men had flashlights. The beam of light reached already the corner of the grit box. To his horror, Toby realized that the men were going to walk along the old track, not along the service road. They would pass right by the grit box!

Even Toby couldn't watch anymore but closed his eyes and hoped for the best. The gravel crunched under the men's feet as they kept coming closer. The duo was discussing quietly.

”...at the same time tomorrow.”

”We can start at one am...”

The men went on their way without noticing the boys. Sons of Night's eyes were maybe closed but its ears were open. And maybe those ears had heard enough.

FOURTEEN

The boys were awakened by a loud rattling coming from above. It sounded like something was rolling along the tin roof.

"What the hell is that?" Toby rubbed his sleepy eyes and tried to force himself into reality. Matty and Marc were going through the same struggle.

It had been almost two am. before Sons of Night had arrived to the hut from its night adventures and sleep hadn't come easily to any of them. They had gone through the events at the factory and speculated about the men's intentions. No one had come up with a sensible explanation for the men being there. Marc had suggested that the men were keen bird watchers and the factory area was home to some rare bird species. Matty and Toby had thought that otherwise it could be possible but Marc hadn't seen those guys in daylight. They hadn't looked like bird watchers, not one bit. The boys had also been remembering the conversation, which they had heard as the men had walked past. They had talked about the forthcoming night and the boys had figured it meant that the men would return to the factory by then. Sons of Night would be there also, the boys had decided before falling asleep.

The roof was rattling again and Willie's voice was heard outside.

"Wakey, wakey!" Willie shouted and threw another cone on the roof of the hut. "Matty's and Marc's parents are already waiting down there in the yard."

"Oh shit!" Matty suddenly remembered. "We were supposed to go to visit Aunt Helen! Today!"

Total chaos broke out in the hut as the brothers tried to hurry, feeling still a little dizzy. Toby watched the situation with amusement. He believed the brothers broke the world record for dressing up. Willie's head appeared in the opening. He warned the brothers that their mother seemed to be in a bad mood. Matty replied that they already knew it from experience. Willie promised to tell the parents that the boys were coming in no time.

After Willie had left, Toby began to talk about the following night and reminded the boys about it. Matty said they wouldn't miss it for the world, but it could be hard to get the permission for another night at the hut. The brothers climbed downstairs and hurried out of the hut. Toby hollered after the duo that he would call later in the day and ask their status.

Mom was waiting for the boys outside the car, with her arms folded, and the brothers prepared for an angry lecture.

"At last! What were you two thinking!" she scolded as the boys got to the car. "Didn't we agree that you would be home at 10:30 at the latest? Just for your information, it's already 11:05."

The boys were looking at their shoes. Mom continued rebuking her sons and asked why they hadn't responded to her calls. The other line had been dead and the other phone had just rang. Matty dug his cell phone out of his pocket and discovered that it had run out of battery. Marc's phone, in turn, had been on silent. Mom still demanded to know why the boys didn't put any alarm on. Matty replied in a quiet voice that they had forgotten because they had had such a fun time.

Dad, who had been sitting quietly in the car, opened the window and said they would be late even more now. Mom ordered the boys to get in the car and jumped in the front seat herself, looking still annoyed. And so the journey to Aunt Helen's began.

Helen was aunt to Mom and therefore great-aunt to the brothers. She lived in a village called Tarheath, which was less than two hundred kilometers to the north of Fort Sara. Her husband,

Benjamin, had passed away a few years ago and nowadays Helen lived alone in a big farmhouse.

At the beginning of the journey, Mom still tried to nag about the boys being late but Dad thought it was enough already. He told Mom to think back her own childhood summers, what had been the best thing: the freedom. Mom didn't say anything on that but gave the brothers in the back seat a comb and a mirror and told them to freshen themselves up. Dad soon informed that because the traffic was so light, they would be just a little late, after all.

In the back seat, the brothers chatted quietly about the coming night. Even though their Mom seemed to have calmed down a bit, the boys thought it would be impossible to get the permission for another night. The duo felt tired after the eventful night and the journey continued quietly.

The clock in the car showed 13:05 when Dad finally parked the car in front of Aunt Helen's house. Mom looked slightly embarrassed noticing that they had arrived only five minutes late. Auntie was in the front yard and smiled brightly as she saw the whole family coming.

"Welcome my dears, it's been such a long time!" Aunt Helen welcomed and embraced all of them. "You arrived just in time! I have just set the table ready."

The boys' great aunt had always been very hospitable and friendly. Matty and Marc kind of liked to visit Aunt even though there was quite boring from time to time. But this time, they would have rather stayed home making plans for the night.

Helen had set the table in the garden under the trees and Mom marveled at the view. Matty and Marc agreed that the view was certainly awesome, but they were thinking mainly the food on the table. At great aunt's home, the table used to be bending under the weight of all kinds of goodies, and in this circumstance, it was more than welcome because the boys hadn't had any breakfast, for obvious reasons.

Karelian pies, egg butter, croissants, cinnamon rolls, biscuits, chocolate, juice, coffee... With eyes wide open, the boys stared at the amount of food on the table and great aunt noticed it. Helen thought, laughing, that the brothers seemed hungry. Mom rushed to explain, as if apologizing, that the boys had missed the breakfast because of the overnight stay in the hut. Helen invited the boys to feel free to eat anything on the table, in any order they like. Matty and Marc didn't need another invitation but immediately dug in.

At the coffee table, the adults discussed about things the boys weren't interested in. Dad also looked a little disinterested from time to time when

Mom and Aunt Helen got carried away thinking back Mom's childhood. Helen had always been talkative and even more now as she lived alone. Having satisfied their hunger, Marc and Matty began to feel bored and tired. Despite her talkativeness, Aunt Helen was attentive and soon noticed the boys' boredom.

"Oh dear! Here we are, chattering about old times."

Helen felt sorry for the boys because she had no toys or anything like that for children as she and Ben had been childless. However, she said that in Ben's workshop in the back yard could be something interesting for the boys. The workshop had been totally Ben's own kingdom and she didn't even know what was in there, really. Helen yet said that everything in the workshop was like Ben had left it. The brothers got enthusiastic about the idea and thanked Helen politely before leaving the table.

The outbuilding, where the workshop was, was located in the back of the garden. At the other end of the building was a sauna with dressing rooms and next to them a shed and the workshop. The boys gently opened the door leading into the workshop. Inside, everything was neatly in order. Only a thin layer of dust on the floor and cobwebs in the corners told that the workshop had been idle for some time. Rows of tools hung nicely above the workbench and the goods on the shelves were in order. Benjamin had undoubtedly been a decent man.

Matty and Marc began to look through the shelves of goods and the workbench drawers. Marc wondered if they could find a football or a frisbee, or even badminton rackets. Matty didn't believe that such things would be found in the workshop. Next, Marc's attention was drawn to the two devices hanging on the back wall.

"What are these?" Marc took the devices from the wall and showed them to Matty.

"Well, they look like phones," pondered Matty. "But they sure aren't cell phones."

The boys decided to take the devices with them and ask Helen.

The parents and Aunt Helen had already left the table. Helen was showing the garden to Mom and Dad seemed to be busy with Aunt's car. Helen had asked Dad to check her car because she herself couldn't.

"Did you find something interesting in there?" Helen asked as the boys came from the workshop.

"These widgets that look like cell phones," Marc showed the devices. "What are these?"

Great aunt quickly recognized the devices as walkie-talkies and explained the boys that Ben had used them in elk hunting. Ben had been a so-called beater who drove elks towards the shooters. Dad had also appeared in the garden to see what the boys had found. Helen thought that Dad would know how to use those walkie-talkies. She promised to give the phones to the brothers even though Mom resisted the idea a bit. Dad also said that those walkie-talkies looked pretty expensive. Helen replied, however, that she wouldn't need them anyway and it would be only good thing if the boys found some use to them. Matty and Marc were grateful and assured that the walkie-talkies would come in handy.

Dad looked at the phones more closely and turned them on from the power switch. A crackle was heard as the walkie talkies came to life. Dad was surprised that the batteries were still working. The boys watched and listened carefully to Dad as he showed them how to use the walkie-talkies. Dad explained also that the walkie-talkie range could reach even a couple of kilometers away, depending on the circumstances.

The boys wanted to try the phones in practice. Dad told the boys to stay in the yard, though, while testing them. Matty suggested that Marc could go behind the house and he himself behind the outbuilding. In that way, there would be two obstacles and a maximum distance between them. The boys set the walkie-talkies in the same frequency and went in their positions. When everything was ready and the boys were in their positions, Matty pushed the push-to-talk button, the PTT, as Dad had called it. Behind the house, Marc's phone crackled and he could hear Matty's voice crystal clear. The boys chit-chatted for a while until they came to the conclusion that the walkie-talkies worked perfectly. Matty's cell phone rang just as the boys had finished their testing. The caller was Toby.

”Matty,” answered Matty with his name.

”Hello, it's Toby. Are you still there, I mean, at your great aunt's?”

”Yeah.”

”Did you get the permission yet?”

”Noup, Mom was so angry that we haven't even tried.”

The boys discussed about the matter and Toby suggested that the brothers could leave from their home. Matty liked the idea and thought it would be the best option. The boys agreed they would do so. Matty told Toby about the walkie-talkies they had got from aunt Helen. Toby thought the phones would be exellent for S.O.N.

”Matthew!” Mom's call interrupted the boys conversation. ”We are leaving soon.”

”Okay, I'm coming,” Matty yelled back and told Toby they were about to leave.

Toby reminded Matty that the brothers' bikes had been left at the hut. Matty said he would ask his Dad to drive via Toby's home. Toby promised to come out so that they could chat a little more about the night.

The others were already ready to leave when Matty came behind the outbuilding.

"What took you so long?" Marc asked.

Matty told Marc that Toby had called and that he would tell more later. Helen said goodbyes to Matty also and then wished them all a safe journey home.

On the way home, Matty explained to Marc in a quiet voice what he and Toby had planned. Marc agreed it was best for them to leave from home. The duo thought the best way for leaving was to sneak out through the window upstairs and climb down the fire escape ladder. Mom began to pay attention to the brothers' whispering in the back seat so the boys decided to discuss more at home. It would be better not to wake any more suspicion.

The boys quieted down and got lost in their thoughts. Soon, Matty noticed that Marc had fallen asleep, head against the window. Matty didn't feel sleepy himself. He was thinking back the events at the factory and tried to figure out what those men were up to. They weren't bird watchers or any other nature lovers that was for sure.

Dad had put the radio on and, despite Mom's protests, listened to some schlager music. After a couple of songs, there was a news broadcast. Matty listened to the radio with half an ear. There was local news at the end of the broadcast.

"And then some regional news," the news reader's voice sounded official. "During the night between Thursday and Friday, a break-in occurred at a building site on Park Street. The burglars stole copper pipes and electric cable. According to police, the burglars had been driving possibly a Ford Transit van with a trailer. Please report any findings to police at..."

A cold shiver went down Matty's spine. The burglars had been driving a Ford Transit van. The news reader's words echoed in his head. Could it be possible? Matty thought. Could it be possible that those were the same guys?

"What's the point of stealing electric cable and pipes or something?" Matty directed the question to his Dad.

"They are made of copper," replied Dad. "It's valuable these days. You can resell the copper at a good price."

Could there be copper at the old factory, Matty wondered frantically. He didn't dare to ask his Dad about that. But the more Matty thought about the news and the men, the more sure he was: those had to be the same guys. Sons of Night was after real criminals!

FIFTEEN

Matty woke up to the beeping sound of his cell phone's alarm. He fought to keep his eyes open as the sleep tried to overtake him. The clock showed five minutes to twelve, just as planned.

The brothers had met Toby shortly after returning from aunt Helen's. The boys had discussed about the coming night and decided that Matty and Marc would leave their home on Stonebridge Road around midnight and would then ride to Toby's home. Toby would be waiting them at Meadow Street. Matty had told Toby and Marc, who had been sleeping during the news, what he had heard. Both the two had agreed with Matty that those guys could very well be the same ones and that they might be stealing copper from the factory. All the members of S.O.N had been excited about this new piece of information and barely could wait until midnight.

In the evening, before going to bed, Marc and Matty had planned their leave more carefully. They had left the gable window ajar. The plan was to sneak out through the window at the end of the corridor and climb down the fire escape ladder to the ground. The boys thought that the weakest point of the plan was the fact that the ladder happened to be also near the parents' bedroom window. On top of that, their Mom was a light sleeper. Mom had seemed to be a little suspicious already in the evening and had told them to go to sleep. The boys had then decided to be even more careful and try to avoid any extra noise. They would sleep in their outerwear and just pull some warm clothes and the sneakers on. Furthermore, just Matty would put the alarm on and then would wake Marc up.

Matty sat on the edge of the bed, yawning. Being awake two nights in a row began to take its toll. He forced himself to get up and pulled on a sweater and the balaclava. Then he sneaked to the door of his room and put the sneakers on his feet. After listening a while, Matty opened the door to the corridor as quietly as he could. The door to Marc's room was on the opposite side of the corridor. Matty was just taking a step towards Marc's door when he heard a whisper coming from the end of the corridor.

"Psst, Matty!" Marc hissed.

Matty glanced in the direction of the voice and saw his brother standing by the window. Avoiding the creaking floor boards, Matty tip-toed along the wall to Marc.

"I see you're already in full gear."

"Yeah, I couldn't get much sleep."

They both had been nervous already in the evening and Matty admitted that he, too, had slept badly. The boys checked that they had everything needed: flashlights, walkie-talkie and Marc's binoculars. They had left the other walkie-talkie to Toby. Everything seemed to be ready for the Son of Night's second patrol.

Cool air flooded into the warm corridor as Matty opened the window. Until then, the boys had managed to move almost silently but the toughest part was still ahead. The lights weren't on in the parent's bedroom but the brothers weren't sure if Mom had fallen asleep yet. Matty suggested that Marc, being smaller, would climb down first. Marc stuck his head out of the window and looked around. The yard and Stonebridge Road behind the hedge seemed quiet. The faint light of the set sun could be seen over the horizon. Marc gathered up his courage and took a deep breath. The heavy scents of early summer floated in the air but, at the moment, there was no time to snif around.

Marc took a tight hold of the window frame and moved his left leg through the window. After kicking in the empty air a couple of times, he managed to reach the fire escape ladder and placed his foot on the rung of the ladder. Slowly, Marc put his weight on his left foot and then swung his body outside the window and grabbed a hold of the ladder with his left hand. Matty watched closely while his little brother balanced his way onto the ladder. But Marc looked so confident that he didn't need to worry. Outside, Marc was already climbing down the ladder and didn't even glance towards the parent's bedroom window.

Upon reaching the ground, Marc raised his thumb to show Matty that everything was okay and then ran, hunched over, to the shelter of the hedge at the border of the yard. After seeing Marc running across the yard safely, Matty got moving right away. Being bigger than Marc, he had to struggle to get through the narrow window but he managed without causing much noise. After getting on the ladder, Matty stopped to listen for a moment. Then, as everything seemed to be okay and the parent's bedroom window remained dark, he climbed nimbly down the ladder and rushed across the yard to his brother.

"Everything OK?" Marc asked briefly.

"Yeah," Matty nodded. "No problems."

The boys crept along the hedge to the carport where their bikes were. The carport wasn't visible from the house so it was quite easy for them to sneak inside and take the bikes out. Silently, the duo jumped on the saddle and headed towards Toby's home.

Ignoring the darkness, the boys rode without lights. They had decided to make a detour to avoid the busiest roads. On weekend, there would probably be more people on the streets and S.O.N didn't want to attract any attention. The detour from Stonebridge Road to Meadow Street was simple. First, along the path through the playground, then to the right along an old bridle path. The bridle path followed the edge of a field and finally ended at a small gravel road which led to Meadow Street.

Matty had turned the walkie-talkie on before leaving. Just when they were about to enter Meadow Street, the phone began to crackle in his pocket and Toby's voice could be heard clearly.

"Broadsword calling Danny boy, Broadsword calling Danny boy. Over."

"What is he playing at now?" Matty wondered, chuckling, and took the phone from his pocket.

He pushed the PTT button and asked Toby what was that crap all about. Toby laughed and explained that it was a line from a movie which he thought was cool.

"Well, don't know about that," Matty replied. "But at least these phones are working fine!"

The brothers continued along Meadow Street and soon saw Toby, who was already waiting for them on the street. Toby had slept in the hut and had come along the path to the street. He complained that it had been a bit creepy to sleep alone in the hut and even creepier to walk through the woods.

"Let's go right away," Toby said as he checked the time on his phone. "We haven't too much time. Those guys were talking about one o'clock."

The full moon had come out from behind the clouds and painted the landscape with an eerie glow as Sons of Night was making its way along the dark streets of Fort Sara. The trio decided to avoid the center of the town and go a slightly longer route to the factory. The boys assumed that the route they had chosen would be quieter. They did manage to get all the way to Fort Sara Road without any problems and were already approaching Ace One, until they saw the first headlights coming. A car approached the trio from behind. The boys made a quick decision to hide behind rose bushes bordering the road. The car whizzed past without slowing down and the boys saw it turning onto the driveway of Ace One. They figured it was just someone who needed gas, and therefore harmless, so they continued their journey towards the factory.

The lights at the Kermia Ltd's main gate shone bright in an otherwise dark and gloomy landscape. This time the boys watched and observed the factory area with new eyes. The lights were burning apparently just because of theft prevention. However, the trio thought that the area was so big that a few lights here and there wouldn't help anything. The thieves could easily break into the area without anyone noticing.

After turning onto Lake Goblin Road, the boys switched the lights on again. Matty thought they already knew the route so well that they could ride even without lights. Marc and Toby laughed that last night they had almost lost their teeth while hitting the potholes, so it wouldn't be wise. By laughing and joking, the boys tried to hide their growing sense of fear.

The factory fence on the right, turn to the right, the railway embankment on the left... Familiar landmarks stood out in the dark and the boys soon arrived at the same place where they had left their bikes the previous night. It was five minutes to half past eleven. The van wasn't behind the embankment and it was dead silent everywhere, so the boys reckoned they had come on time.

The trio held a short negotiation.

"Let's hide the bikes here and walk to the same place where we were yesterday," Toby suggested.

"What if the men walk along the embankment, like yesterday?" Marc asked worried. "They'll see us behind that grit box for sure."

Both Matty and Toby replied that those guys wouldn't walk if they were going to steal copper and other stuff. They would drive through the gate and go inside the area.

"Besides," Matty added. "We would hear them coming."

The boys managed to convince Marc that it was safe to hide behind the box and so the trio headed towards the crossing.

The last clouds in the sky had drifted away as S.O.N reached the crossing and took position behind the grit box. To the delight but also to the dismay of the boys, the moon lit up the landscape surprisingly bright. On the other hand, they could see all the way to the rail yard but, on the other hand, the boys felt they were exposed in the open area.

Toby wanted to make sure they weren't seen from the road. He asked Matty to go to the road and check if he could see him and Marc behind the box. Matty went on his way and soon informed by walkie-talkie that if he didn't know the boys were there, he wouldn't see them. However, if Toby or Marc moved a bit, he could see the movement right away. Toby told Matty to come back because the men could come any minute. The trio sat behind the grit box and waited.

The minutes seemed to crawl by and the seeds of doubt began to grow in everyone's mind. What if they had imagined the whole thing? What if the men were just some bird watchers after all? Even though the boys were dressed warmly, they started to shiver from cold after being motionless for minutes. Alternately, all the members of S.O.N thought they were hearing an engine sound or seeing something, but each time it turned out to be just imagination.

Once again, the boys became alerted. Now they all heard it at the same time. A car! No doubt about it! First muffled, then louder, until the boys could see the headlights glowing eerily between the trees. The car came along the service road towards the boys. The trio kept their heads down as the car came into sight. The driver slowed down and turned the car towards the rail yard gate.

"It's the guard!" Toby whispered as he peeked from behind the box. "Exactly at the same time as yesterday!"

The guard did the same routines at the gate as the night before and then continued his round.

"I wonder what's going to happen next?" Marc put everyone's thoughts into words.

Would anything happen? Would the men, driving the red Ford Transit, come up also? Sons of Night waited, cheered by the visit of the guard. A minute passed, and then another. Nothing was heard nor seen. The trio waited quietly, not moving an inch.

Just when Toby was about to scold them all being a bunch of idiots who have seen too many movies, things began to happen fast.

Somewhere nearby an engine was started. A sudden fear gripped the boys's hearts because the sound of the engine was scarily familiar. The knocking sound of a diesel couldn't be mistaken. The suspicious men were on the move again.

"Be careful and vigilant now!" wheezed Toby anxiously.

The revs of the van's engine got higher as the driver changed down. Soon, the Transit's headlights swept the trees the same way as the lights of the security patrol car moments earlier. This time the trio kept their heads down long before the van appeared in sight. Sons of Night sensed it was the real thing now. The van approached the crossing of the old railway and the service road and, for a moment, the boys thought it would hit the grit box. The forest behind the boys' hiding place was lit by the headlights of the van as it turned towards the rail yard. Then it became completely dark again.

It took a few seconds before the eyes got used to the dark again. The boys carefully raised their heads to see what was happening. The van was idling in front of the gate and behind it was a big trailer with canopy on top. The door on the passenger's side opened and a man jumped out of the van and strode briskly to the gate. Toby and Matty recognized the man as the tattooed binocular guy. Without hesitation, the man cut the chain with a heavy-duty bolt cutters and opened the doors. Petrified, the boys watched the events from their hiding place as if they were watching an action movie.

The binocular man, who had opened the gate, returned to the van which drove straight away through the gate and headed towards the warehouses. The boys couldn't believe what was happening.

”This can't be real!” Matty said with a trembling voice. ”I must be dreaming.”

”Then we all are,” Toby replied. ”But I think we are witnessing a real burglary here!”

”What are we going to do now?” Marc's voice sounded frantic with fear. ”Should we call the police?”

The boys discussed quickly about the situation. Toby wanted to wait and see how things would develop before calling, Matty wasn't sure and Marc was too terrified to think rationally. The van had stopped in front of the first warehouse and the men had already come out of the cockpit. The boys tried to see what the men were doing. But even though there was a full moon and the lights in the yard, the warehouses were too far away. Toby suggested that they would go closer to take a look. Marc refused absolutely but Matty said he would go. The two suggested that Marc could wait behind the box. However, Marc said he wouldn't stay there if the two were leaving. He would rather come along than sit alone in the dark.

So, the trio jumped from behind the grit box and, hunched over, ran towards the gate. They decided to go behind the collapsed gatekeeper's lodge. From that distance they might be able to see something. None of the boys wanted to go inside the fenced area, after all, so behind the pile of boards was the closest safe place.

Matty remembered that the boards were full of rusty nails sticking out in every direction. He warned Toby and Matty about it as the boys took positions behind the pile. The men in the factory area had somehow managed to open one of the doors leading inside the warehouse and were apparently already inside the building, at least the boys could no longer see them. The canopy on top of the trailer was open. The trio tried to peer at the warehouse but it was still too far away.

"Oh," Marc suddenly whispered. "Just remembered that I took the binoculars along."

"And only now you're telling us," Toby scolded.

"Actually," Matty defended his little brother. "I was also aware of the binoculars and didn't remember to tell."

Toby waved his hand vaguely, replying that it didn't matter anymore. He wanted to use the binoculars himself and the brothers had nothing against it. Toby raised the binoculars to his eyes and explained what he was seeing. The door to the warehouse was open, so was the canopy on top of the trailer, but the men he couldn't see anywhere. Matty got angry and said they could see all that even without the binoculars. There was nothing else to see, claimed Toby. Suddenly, all three saw even with bare eyes that some lights were flashing inside the warehouse. Immediately after that, was heard a muffled clattering as if some metal pipes had fallen on a stone floor. Then began a high-pitched buzzing and Toby informed he saw some sparking.

"What the hell is going on in there?" Toby wondered.

"That's a sound of an angle grinder," replied Matty. "They're cutting something."

Toby and Matty glanced at each other meaningly.

"Copper pipes!" the two realized it at the same time.

"Well, can we call the police now?" Marc insisted.

Neither of the boys didn't have time to reply before one of the men stepped out of the warehouse, carrying something in his arms. The man had a bright headlamp on his head. Toby watched closely with the binoculars to find out what the guy was up to.

"That guy is carrying metal pipes!" Toby whispered, tension in his voice. "I can't see if they are copper pipes, though."

It was obvious that the men had different assignments. The other cut the pipes shorter inside the warehouse and the other carried them right away in the trailer. Toby recognized the man carrying the pipes as the van's driver. The duo worked promptly and professionally. For a while, Sons of Night watched silently and made observations as the men kept on working. Finally, Marc cut the silence and again insisted on calling the police. Toby was still a little skeptical and was still thinking of some option other than burglary. Marc pleaded with his big brother to agree with him. They had all seen how the men broke through the gate. Matty admitted that it had looked like a break-in but he himself wouldn't dare to make a call to emergency number.

The trio's discussion was stopped by a loud bang from the warehouse. Both men were now in the yard and the bang was due to shutting the canopy. The man, who had loaded the trailer, jumped into the cockpit and drove the van in front of the next door. The tattooed guy, who had used the angle grinder, marched behind on foot.

"That tattooed dude has a crowbar!" Toby had begun to watch with the binoculars again and told the boys what he was seeing.

"It seems like he's prying the door open with it," Toby sounded both breathless and excited.

The man worked hard with the door for a moment until the lock gave way and the door flew open with a clatter. Now also Toby was ready to admit that they were dealing with real criminals here. The boys decided it was time to call for help because the situation was becoming too dangerous for Sons of Night. Toby volunteered to call to the emergency number and the brothers thought Toby would be the best for the job. However, Matty feared that the person answering the call might identify the caller being a child. Toby said he was going to keep his sleeve in front of the cell phone and would also try to lower his voice. The boys decided to take the risk because something had to be done anyway.

Toby went straight into action. He cleared his throat a couple of times, dialled the emergency number and lifted the phone to his ear. Matty and Marc listened with bated breath as Toby started to speak in a low voice through his sleeve.

"Hello! We were just driving along Lake Goblin Road in Fort Sara. There was some strange lights in the factory area, you know, that old Kermia factory..."

The brothers admired their friend's performance. Toby sounded really convincing even though he was just making up the story as he went along.

"Yeah, beams from flashlights or something and they were moving in the rail yard. It's closed factory anyway, no one supposed to be there..." Toby continued his story. "So, if you could send a patrol unit there to check it. Yeah! Sorry, have to hang up, my battery is dying. Bye!"

After the call was over, Toby took a deep breath and told the boys that he had finished the call when the woman at the other end had begun to inquire his name. Matty and Marc praised Toby for doing an impressive job. The boys were sure that a patrol unit would come to check the situation.

In the meantime, the burglars had continued their job. The driver was going inside the warehouse and the tattooed crowbar man was just carrying a big coil in the back of the van. Toby was watching with the binoculars and told the boys that the coil was a cable roll. Matty mentioned about the radio news he had heard earlier, there had been told that the burglars stole pipes and electric cables also. The trio became more and more convinced of the fact that those were the same thieves.

The men carried more and more cable rolls out of the warehouse. Marc glanced at his watch and worried what was taking so long for the police. Fifteen minutes had already passed since the call.

Toby, too, became worried when he noticed that the van was almost full.

Soon it became clear that the burglars, indeed, were about to leave. The boys realized that the police wouldn't arrive in time. Sons of Night had to come up with something, and fast!

SIXTEEN

In front of the warehouse, the Transit's side door slammed shut. Panic began to grow among the boys. Something had to be done or else the burglars would get away. But what? What could three kids possibly do in a situation like this? At least they had to get away from the gate or else they would certainly be seen. To the boys' horror, they already heard the engine starting.

"Come on, let's go! Now!" Marc shouted in panic.

At that very moment, Matty got an idea.

"Let's puncture their tires!"

Toby understood immediately what Matty had in mind. Nails! There was a pile of boards full of nails right in front of them. Matty was already one step ahead and was searching a suitable board from the pile. He told Marc to watch the burglars and Toby to help with the board.

"We'll put the board on the road so that the nails stick straight up, right?" Toby confirmed Matty's thought.

"Exactly," Matty replied. "It's like a spike strip."

The boys found a board with nails they thought would be perfect. Matty told Marc to warn as soon as the burglars were coming. Marc tried to get himself together and watched the rail yard without blinking his eyes. The van was already moving but the men had trouble turning it around with the trailer.

Matty and Toby jumped onto the road and put the board lengthwise on the tire path. Suddenly, the boys realized that the board would be visible from the van and because of the heavy cargo, it would drive slowly. The men would surely notice the board. The duo was already about to reject the idea when Toby came up with another one. He figured that if they spread some gravel on top of the board it could work out. Maybe then the men wouldn't see the board or the nails. Quickly, the two began to scrape loose gravel from the side of the road.

"They are coming right now!" Marc's voice broke with fear.

The men had managed to turn the van around and were slowly approaching the gate, behind which Matty and Toby were setting the trap. The boys scraped frantically more gravel on top of the board and hastily leveled the surface.

"Come on!" Marc shouted desperately as he himself began to run away.

The two other Sons of Night escaped only just before Transit's headlights beam would have reached them. The boys managed to just barely hide behind the grit box when the driver decided to switch to high beams. Suddenly, it was bright all around. The trio had reached the box at the last possible second.

The van seemed to speed up as it was approaching the gate. The boys laid behind the box and didn't dare to move. The rumbling sound of the van kept coming closer and closer. With their nerves strained to the limit, the trio waited. Why didn't anything happen? Wouldn't the van drive over the board? Suddenly, there was a loud bang and the headlights swung over the trees. The boys hold their breath. Maybe their trick had worked, after all. The van's engine failed or was shut off and the doors were opened. The boys heard the men swearing as they stepped out of the cockpit.

"God dammit!" The other of the two raged. "The front tire is blown out!"

"There was a fucking board or something! I noticed it too late," the driver complained. "Fortunately, we have a spare tire. And fortunately there was only one puncture."

"Fortunately and fortunately," the other one continued raging. "We didn't need this! And where did the board come from in the first place? It surely wasn't there when we came."

Behind the grit box, the boys got chills. What if the men come to the conclusion that someone must have put the board on the road? What if they start to look around? Toby was in an awkward position and carefully tried to move his body. At that moment, a short cracking sound was heard, cutting the silence of the night. It felt like it could have been heard miles away. The sound had come from the walkie-talkie in Tobys's pocket. Unfortunately, Toby had left it on and when he changed his position, the PTT button went down.

"Did you hear that?" the driver had, indeed, heard the sound. "It came from the front."

Fucking fuck, Toby berated himself quietly. Now what? They were desperately trapped behind the box. Matty, who was lying next to Toby, signaled with his eyes that they should run for their lives. Toby nodded in understanding. On the other side, Marc was lying with his eyes closed. Matty tugged at his brother's sleeve and tried to get Marc to understand their intentions. Also Marc seemed to realize the situation even though he looked like he was close to tears.

All at once, the boys jumped up and started to run, as fast as they could, along the track towards the forest. From the corner of their eyes, they saw how the shorter of the men was already coming towards the grit box with his headlamp on. The man started cursing heavily as he saw the boys running away and immediately went running after them.

In panic, the boys ran along the dark railway embankment. They were maybe fifty meters ahead of the chasing man. The darkness was on the boys' side but the man would catch them before long anyway. Toby, being the unfittest of the boys, slowly began to fall behind Matty and Marc. He was just about to shout to the brothers that he would give up when he heard something familiar. The rippling of a stream! Toby's despair turned to hope. He quickly told the brothers to stop and motioned them to go down the bank. Matty understood immediately what Toby was thinking. The old culvert! They could hide in there! Matty pulled Marc, who seemed to be too confused to act, down the bank and the duo groped their way through the dark thicket towards the stream. Toby followed right behind them.

Branches scratched the boys' faces but they didn't have time to feel any pain. They had to find a way down to the stream, and fast. Suddenly, the trio realized they had fallen into an icy water which reached almost to their knees. At that moment, it felt like the best feeling in the world. Without hesitation, they waded along the ice-cold stream into the culvert. Toby was leaning on his knees, exhausted, and tried to get his breath back. Matty put a finger in front of his mouth, signaling them to keep very quiet. This would be their last chance.

Headlamp's bright light gleamed from above and the gravel rustled as the burglar ran above the boys' heads and carried on without stopping. Inside the culvert, the trio waited, their heart beating hard, fearing that the man would spot them at any moment. Minute after minute went by. No one dared to move a muscle, nor felt the coldness of the water.

Then the boys saw the gleam of light again but this time from another direction. The burglar came back! And this time the man was walking slowly and seemed to be looking at both sides of the embankment. When he was opposite the stream, he stopped, stood still for a while and then directerd his light down into the darkness. In the culvert, the three boys were terrified. However, it seemed like the man was just randomly looking around the bushes.

"I know that you are somewhere down there!" The man suddenly roared. "Come out or I'll come get you!"

Sons of Night didn't move one bit. The boys realized the guy had absolutely no idea that they were directly below him.

"Let them go!" the other burglar shouted angrily in the distance. "They're just kids!"

The man, who had chased the boys, was muttering something under his breath and then started to walk back to the van. S.O.N down in the culvert sighed in relief. They had survived. The trio waited for a moment, wondering, what would happen next. Would the burglars get away after all?

Suddenly, a sound of an engine was heard from the service road again. This time it wasn't the Transit, though, and it seemed to be driving towards the rail yard. The police! A warm sense of relief flooded through the boys. It had to be the police. No one else would be driving there at night.

All of a sudden, a police siren whooped briefly and blue lights began to flash against the dark sky. What a wonderful sound and what an awesome sight it was! The water of the stream was splashing around as the boys rushed out of the culvert and climbed rapidly up the bank. They wanted to see how the situation would end.

Once again, the three boys walked quietly along the embankment. As they reached the curve, they saw the police patrol car with its lights flashing. The car sat in the middle of the crossing so that it blocked the road. It seemed that the police had arrived in the nick of time. The burglars had changed the tire and had managed to get the van moving again. The boys didn't dare to walk any closer but stayed inside the forest and watched the events.

The police car's back door was open and the other burglar sat handcuffed on the backseat. Two police officers were just walking the tattooed one to the patrol car. Apparently, the man had tried to escape by foot. The boys watched the scene in disbelief, but elated at the same time. Had they really caught the burglars? All the twists and turns taking place during the last hour seemed unreal.

Both burglars were now arrested and the officers put police tape around the van and the trailer. After completing their work, the officers yet looked around for a while and then drove off with the burglars.

Suddenly, it was dark and quiet again. The boys wondered about the strange events for a moment until realizing how tired and soaked they were and only wanted to snuggle up in the warm bed. However, Toby wanted to do one thing before leaving. He had made "a business card" for Sons of Night and wanted to leave it on the scene.

"This is just a little reminder that Sons of Night was here," Toby laughed as he pulled the card from his pocket.

The brothers thought it was a great idea. They decided to put the card on the Transit's windshield.

Sons of Night left the scene but also left a strict message behind:

"When the rest are sleeping, Sons of Night is awake."

<h1 style="text-align:center">SEVENTEEN</h1>

"Matthew and Marcus, it's time to get up already!" Mom's voice came from the stairs and sounded demanding. "It's almost midday!"

It had been not until half past two when the brothers had come home at night and getting to sleep had been difficult after the exciting mission. Matty thought he had fallen asleep just shortly before four.

Mom's voice had broken into his sleep but he found it hard to open his eyes. Only when he heard approaching footsteps in the corridor and a knock at the door, he woke up. In panic, Matty threw his dirty sneakers and clothes under his bed, and not a moment too soon. Mom opened the door and peeked into the room with an inquiring expression on her face.

"Did you sleep at all when you were in the hut?" she asked. "You have slept around the clock!"

Matty didn't feel like explaining anything but sat up on the edge of the bed. Fortunately, Mom left to Marc's room without waiting for an answer. Matty hoped that Marc had understood to put his clothes away. He listened for a while if Mom would start yelling but nothing happened. Mom was already going back downstairs, informing that breakfast was still served even though it was lunch time already.

After getting up and dressed, Matty went to look for his brother. Marc was already up and came from his room looking tired and his hair all tangled. Marc told he had had a close call with Mom also. Marc had woken only when Mom was already knocking on Matty's door. His wet and dirty clothes had been all over the floor and he had to throw them in the closet. The brothers laughed at their close calls and thought back over the eventful night. It seemed so unreal, almost like a dream.

The boys decided to go for breakfast before Mom would lose her temper completely. Just then was heard a familiar cracking sound from Matty's room, and immediately after Toby's secret agent type of voice.

"Broadsword calling Danny Boy, Broadsword calling Danny Boy. Over."

Matty shook his head, amused, but went to answer the phone anyway.

"Well, what is it now?" Matty grunted as he pushed the PTT button. "We just woke up and haven't even had any breakfast yet."

Toby sounded mysterious and said he had news regarding last night. He told the boys to eat quickly and then come to the hut. Matty didn't bother to ask further but said they would try to come as soon as possible.

After having a quick breakfast of cereals and juice, the boys headed to the hut. The sun was shining from a cloudless sky. The day was going to be hot again. Toby was waiting them outside, in the cool shade of the hut. He had that same mysterious smile on his face again which told he had something to tell.

"Okay, spit it out!" Matty wasn't in the mood of playing guessing games.

Toby told he had also slept late and went then to breakfast. Willie had still been in the kitchen, drinking coffee. He had heard from the radio that there had been a break-in at Kermia during the night. The police had arrested two men for stealing copper. Willie had been so excited about it that Toby had almost burst into laughter. He had to act as if it was news to him too. There had been told also that the police had received an anonymous tip about the burglary.

The brothers were amazed that the burglary was already on the news. The trio wondered if the police had found their business card already. They laughed that it could be quite a surprise. Matty suggested they should celebrate Sons of Night's first succesful mission. The two other members agreed and the trio decided to go to Ace One again.

On the way, the boys thought back the amazing events at night. Matty and Toby remembered, amused, how Marc had screamed in panic. They laughed also at Toby's getaway run. Toby said it had felt just like in his dream a couple of days before.

At the crossing of Fort Sara Road and Borough Street, the boys heard a car honk from behind. An old Saab stopped beside them at the bus stop. It was Frank the Janitor.

"Hello boys! Where you're going?" Frank shouted as he rolled the window down.

"To Ace One," Toby replied. "Why?"

The boys stayed to listen what Frank had in mind.

"About that vandalism at the school yard, Frank started. "I thought that this might interest you."

Frank told that the police had called him that morning, telling that they had caught the perpetrators. The night before, the police had bumped into two riders who had overspeeded. They were Zac and Archie. By coincidence, the police officers were the same who had checked the school. They had noticed immediately that the tire patterns matched to the tracks found in the school yard. After a little interrogation, Zac and Archie had admitted that they were behind the vandalism.

"That duo is going to get a hard conviction," Frank said, looking almost sad.

The boys, however, weren't terribly sorry after hearing the news, especially not Toby, whom the Monkey Twins had caused enough trouble over the years.

Just when Frank was about to leave, a familiar voice was heard behind the boys.

"What are you doing in the middle of the road?" Fanny was rolling towards the boys with her rollator. "Oh my goodness!"

"Well, I guess I'll be leaving now, bye!" Frank winked his eye and turned the car back on the road.

The boys were left alone at the mercy of Fanny. Quickly, the trio moved to the side of the road and politely gave way for the old lady.

"Please, feel free to proceed, Mrs Fowler," said Toby in an overly sweet voice. "Sons of Night is watching after you!"

The boys erupted in laughter as Fanny went on her way, snorting and grumbling. Sons of Night had the last word but its story continues.